I0558925

breath

and other stories

SILVERTON BOOKS, LOS ANGELES

© Terry Wolverton, 2011
Cover image, ©iStockphoto.com/VikaValter

Silverton Books
c/o Writers At Work
4022 Fountain Avenue, Suite 202
Los Angeles, CA 90029

ISBN 978-0-9629528-6-9
1. Fiction—short stories. 2. Lesbians—Fiction. I. Terry Wolverton

These are works of fiction. Names, characters, places, and incidents either are the product of the author's imagination or are used fictitiously, and any resemblance to actual persons, living or dead, events or locales is entirely coincidental.

for my writing students

acknowledgments

"Breath" was previously published in *Crab Orchard Review*, 2003.

"Outside of Town" was previously published in *Hurricane Alice*, Vol. 8, No. 3, Winter 1991.

"Twenty-nine Palms" was previously published in *Rohwedder*, Issue #6, 1991.

"News" was previously published in *The Stinging Fly*, Winter 2001.

"Temperance" was previously published in *The Crucifix is Down*, Red Hen Press, 2005.

"A Whisper in the Veins" was previously published in *Glimmer Train Stories*, issue #4, Fall 1992.

"Sex Less" was previously published in *Hers 2,* Faber and Faber, 1997.

"Garage Sale" was previously published in *Lovers,* edited by Amber Coverdale Sumrall, The Crossing Press, 1992.

"What Annie Said" was previously published in *Sheila-na-gig*, Vol. III, 1991.

"The Arc of Plot" was previously published in *Circa 2000: Lesbian Fiction At the Millennium*, Alyson Publications, 2000.

"Lifelong" was previously published in *Best Lesbian Love Stories*, Alyson Publications, 2002.

"Evalina's Prayer" was previously published in *Press*, Issue #6, Fall 1997.

contents

breath

Our families always thought we spoiled Madrigal, but both Josh and I were committed to giving our daughter the space she needed to become herself without a lot of interference on our parts. I think it's a value common to our generation, which spent our youths in rebellion against our parents' repression and conformity, and which prized freedom above all else. It is this freedom we tried to give our children.

While our friends' children experimented with drugs or alternative sexual lifestyles, Madrigal's investigations were most often conducted in the alimentary realm. We were of course permissive with her, bemused by her vegetarianism, stoic through her macrobiotic phase. We suffered quietly through the years when our windowsills were crowded with glass jars of hairy looking bean sprouts, and finally resigned ourselves to her regimen of nothing but raw fruits and vegetables, except for oranges, which she would not touch.

We made room on the kitchen counters for the parade of food processors, nut grinders, and Champion juicers she would periodically drag home from her various sojourns: at the ashram, the Himalayan trek, the Zen retreat. We stopped shaking our heads over the baggies of exotic spices that crowded the cabinets, eventually driving out the humble cinnamon and paprika, the banal black pepper. And we no more than sighed at the drying racks that colonized our oven, thin metal bars layered with flattened disks of tomato, apricot, their soft flesh leathering.

Even as a little girl, Madrigal was different than our friends' children. She wasn't interested in Barbies or Nintendo or TV or riding her bike. She never seemed to want to hang out with kids her own age. From the time she was six or seven, she spent a lot of her time alone in her room; she could sit for hours on her bed, smiling and humming to herself. When we asked her what she was doing, she'd say, "talking to God" or "singing with the angels." This surprised us, because both Josh and I had fallen away from our faiths–Jewish and Methodist, respectively. Madrigal had never set foot in church or temple.

"Do you think it's weird?" Josh asked me, of our daughter's spontaneous devotion. Like many of our generation, we were suspicious of religion, which we viewed as a form of social control.

"Actually, I think it's kind of sweet," I told him. We stood at the open door of her room. "Look at her." And indeed, our golden haired daughter's face was radiant as she sang to a spirit we could not see.

Josh's mother thought there was something wrong with Madrigal. "It's not normal," she said time and time again. "You need to take her to a psychiatrist, get her tested. I think she's autistic." Widowed when Josh was in his early teens, my mother-in-law was an amateur therapist; she'd read every self-help book in print and was never shy about offering her diagnosis. His mother's unsolicited advice may have been the very thing that convinced him that our only child was perfect.

"She's fine, Ma," he would dismiss her in that tone of impatience that only surfaced when he talked to his mother. "Leave her alone."

Our daughter was always a picky eater. She would eat only what she liked and she only liked a discrete number of things. At age five, she rejected meat, a stance that secretly delighted me; I too had declared myself a vegetarian at age sixteen, provoking severe battles with my father at the dinner table. I'd lapsed since being married, but I was more than willing to celebrate this impulse in my daughter. She had her own set of dietary rules, her own strict orthodoxy. Tuna fish sandwiches were fine, but only if the tuna was mixed with lemon juice, not mayonnaise, and never if the mixture included sweet relish. She liked grilled cheese sandwiches, but only on rye bread and with a little catsup, but it had to be Heinz or else she would leave the whole thing to congeal in its buttery coat.

"You're spoiling her rotten," my mother chastised us for indulging her, but the truth was, if Madrigal didn't find the food to her liking she would simply refuse to eat for as long as her preference was denied. Not just hours, but days.

"Come on, baby girl, just try this chicken," I'd brightly encourage, "Just a couple of bites, okay?"

Her eyes would grow sad. "It's a bird," she'd protest, as if I'd failed to grasp this essential thing. What kind of barbarian was I, I'd wonder to myself, trying to cajole my daughter into eating a creature with wings?

She never threw a tantrum or got angry. She simply abstained. She would sit at the table, her plate empty before her, and give us pitying glances as we spooned up whatever she had disdained. I used to think she kept a secret cache of food in her room, but we never found anything, not a wrapper, not a crumb, to betray her. Her preferences were so pronounced and her will so unshakeable that we decided it was better to simply give her what she wanted. Maybe if she'd only wanted candy bars we would have intervened more. But tuna and grilled cheese? Apples and bananas? How could we complain?

"I'd make her eat and like it," my father once growled, when he was still alive, but he was from a different generation with different ideas about child rearing. I remembered the whippings I would get if I protested that I didn't like brussels sprouts or fried liver, and the hours of being forced to sit at the table, my bottom still stinging, my face flushed with shame and injustice. Sometimes I sat well into the night while everyone else went to bed, forced to remain there until my plate was cleaned.

Josh and I met in college in 1970. It's a cliché but we actually met at an anti-war demonstration. This was a time when we believed the world could change and that our generation would be the ones to change it. After we fell in love, we used lie on my mattress with the batik print sheets and talk about the child we'd have together. We both wanted only one child, because we didn't want to contribute to overpopulation. We both wanted a girl, Josh because he didn't want to have a son "to feed the war machine."

"We won't ever spank her." Josh would say.

"Never!" I agreed, "She'll grow up knowing only peace and love."

"And when she's old enough, she'll have a say in what the household rules are." He'd pass a lighted joint in my direction and I'd suck the smoke into my lungs, feel it wash over my limbs like spirit.

"And we won't hassle her about her hair," I'd exhale, "or what she wants to wear."

"And no TV. No junk food."

"But what if she wants that?"

"She won't, baby, she won't. She'll know how empty and corrupt all that is."

"I love you, Joshua Lehrman." And then I'd roll on top of him, and we'd go back to making love, trying things we'd read about in the copy of the *Kama Sutra* I kept stashed beneath the mattress.

Madrigal was in junior high school when she made the declaration that she was no longer going to eat any "other animals." That was how she put it. No more tuna. "Nothing with a face," she'd say. She had already begun to dress only in white clothing, winter or summer. I remembered my own high school years–miniskirts and bell-bottoms, halter-tops–and was obliging. In truth I was relieved she hadn't gone for the black leather and heavy boots, the metal studs in every orifice that so many of our friends' children adopted. I was less sanguine when she shaved off her beautiful golden curls and had a mandala tattooed on the top of her head. Still, her face was lovely and in a way, the starkness became her; she seemed all the more striking. In her snowy gauze fabrics, with her shaved head, she seemed to emanate a kind of glow.

It was during these years that our friends started to complain about their offspring. "Liana is always on the phone; my boss couldn't even get through last night!" "Jordan won't get off my computer." "Eric is constantly after me to buy the latest video game; man, those things are expensive." "Meadow came home and her eyes looked funny, but I couldn't get her to tell me what she was on." And all of them, it seemed, were always going off with their friends to god knew where and didn't come back until the wee hours of the morning.

Josh and I marveled at how easy we had it. Madrigal went to school, came home, meditated in her room. "How was school?" I'd ask her, as she drifted in the back door. I was selling real estate in those days, and I worked from home. She'd give me a brilliant smile that seemed to contain both mystery and wonder. Once in a while I'd coax her to tell me something about her day, but it was never about girlfriends or boys she was interested in or bands she liked to listen to–the kinds of things I talked about at thirteen. She'd say, "They made us cut open a frog in biology class today. I wanted to leave but I had to stay. I just watched the way his heart pumped, and I could feel my own heart pumping right along with him." Or she'd say, "Our music teacher played us

Barber's Adagio for Strings and it made me feel like I was rocking on a boat somewhere at night."

Sometimes I wondered if she was lonely, but she never showed any sign of it; she seemed deeply content. I began to harbor the secret fantasy that she really was special, perhaps a saint in the making. I wasn't sure what Josh and I had done to deserve such a gift, but I was grateful.

I had a hard time imagining my daughter in high school, drifting through the halls like a Hollywood version of a Tibetan monk, floating slightly above the scarred linoleum on her way to class. I couldn't envision her at her locker, or in PE. I couldn't picture her in algebra or gossiping with a friend in the cafeteria. It was a while before I learned that in fact my daughter didn't actually attend the private high school we'd so carefully lobbied to get her into and for which we had paid tens of thousands of dollars. I learned that she left the house each morning in her white wide-legged Indian cotton pants or the long white tube skirt she'd crocheted herself. She took her backpack, which I had always assumed contained books. She'd flash me her detached, dazzling smile and close the door behind her, then spend the day wandering the city.

The school was as progressive as we could find; many of the students had parents in the entertainment industry who often went off for months to shoot in exotic locations and took their kids along. It was several weeks before the school thought to communicate with us about our daughter's absence.

When the headmaster finally called me, I tried to make excuses for my daughter. "Maybe she doesn't find school that challenging," I suggested.

"That's the trouble with the Baby Boom generation," his voice was indignant. "You grew up resisting authority, and now you can't exercise it over your own children. Children need discipline…" It was an odd line of argument from the director of an alternative school; he was close to a decade younger than I, "a product of the Reagan era," as I would later sniff to Josh. I cut him off, mid-lecture.

"Let me talk to Madrigal," I said coldly, "and I will call you back."

When confronted, she made neither excuses nor apologies. "No," she smiled gently, as if we'd asked a very stupid question, but it wasn't our fault. "I don't go to school."

"But where do you go?" Josh demanded.

She answered without a trace of defensiveness. "Sometimes I go to the park and talk to the old people who sit there all day. Or I go to the library. Sometimes I read to people at the hospital. On Wednesdays I'll go to the farmer's market and buy a lot of apples and bananas and then go downtown and hand them out to people who live on the streets."

"You hang out on Skid Row?" Josh's voice crept dangerously up the register. "With the homeless?" I shot him a glance that said, Cool it.

"They're just people, like anybody," our daughter insisted. It was what we'd taught her, and her clear gaze made us feel ashamed and conflicted. This was our sixteen-year-old daughter, skipping school. Not just a class here or there, but skipping it entirely. But not to smoke pot or meet boys at the shopping mall. Instead of going to school she read to sick people, gave fruit to people who lived in cardboard boxes on the sidewalk. She had created a separate life about which we knew nothing. It was infuriating and terrifying and moving and humbling all at the same time. I was not going to be the person who told her that learning algebraic formulas was more important than what she was doing. I had memorized them all and never in my life since had I had occasion to use them. Those old formulas floated amidst my brain cells, unrecovered, like detritus drifting in outer space.

So we applied to have her "home schooled." We hired a tutor with the instructions that he was to leave her alone, just file the paperwork as needed to satisfy the requirements. When it came time to take her GED, she passed without difficulty. It gave Josh and me a kind of thrill; we felt like we were radicals again, protecting our daughter against the intrusions of the kapitalist state.

Madrigal was no more adapted to college than to high school. "Have you thought about where you'd like to go?" Josh asked her one night. He was always a little nervous talking to her, as if he felt slightly ridiculous in her presence.

She looked amused, though in a kind way. "I don't think that's where I need to be," she said simply.

Of course the work world seemed equally out of the question. Madrigal in an office? Waitressing? Selling cosmetics in the department store or office supplies over the phone?

When Josh's mother died she left a trust for Madrigal. It was supposed to come to her when she married, but we were the trustees and when she turned eighteen we decided to let her have it. Our daughter began traveling then, for weeks or months. Although we fretted about her, out on her own, we were glad to see her make her way in the world. We would get postcards once in a while–from Nepal or Nova Scotia, or Caracas–but she would always come home to our house, to her room that was painted a deep saffron, and which contained no bed, only a thick carpet on the floor. It was surprising, I think, that she returned to us, when all of our friends' children had long since fled the nest. Surprising, a bit worrisome, yet precious, an incalculable gift. My neighbor Andrea's children weren't speaking to her; our daughter still considered our house her home.

If we coaxed hard she would tell us fragments of stories from her travels:

Tibet: "There was one little girl, maybe about eight, her waist was no bigger around than my thigh. But when I handed her a bowl of rice, she gave me the biggest smile."

Zimbabwe: "They don't have medicines like they do here. The doctor would sometimes get so frustrated, and then get on the phone and start yelling at his friends in the States to send more boxes of whatever he needed."

Guatemala: "There were fifteen of us and we'd get up before dawn and go out with our shovels to start digging, because by eight in the morning it was too hot to work."

She was always sparing with the details, as if she wanted to protect us from the harsher realities she faced, and deeply modest, talking about the accomplishments of the others she worked with. They never had names, though; it was always "the doctor" or "the teacher" she referred to, as if she did not relate to them in a personal way.

And each time she would return with some new habit of eating, some new regimen, a new theory of purification. After one such trip, our house was redolent for weeks with the scent of sautéed ginger and garlic, essential, apparently, for healing the lining of the stomach. After another, we could always find dried apricots soaking in a bowl; she would drink the water to "re-mineralize" the body. Such practices were apparently good for her; her skin was clear and radiant, her body lithe. And she never tried to impose her habits on us, although occasionally if she wandered into the kitchen when I was mixing ground beef for a meatloaf or dressing lamb chops, her eyes would fill and she would quietly leave the room.

I didn't know how to talk to my friends about her. When I'd see them at the market, or run into them at a café in town, their conversations were laden with news of their children: "Liana is pregnant with twins." "Jordan just signed a two-book deal." I didn't know how to say, "Madrigal is on a wheat-grass juice fast," or "My daughter is now meditating six hours a day!" or even "My daughter is feeding beggars in Calcutta."

"I supposed we can forget about grandchildren," Josh said to me one night, a little glumly. I could only shrug in response. Did Madrigal have boyfriends? Or, for that matter, girlfriends? Did she ever yearn for someone's particular touch? Did she experiment with positions, techniques, as Josh and I had done when we were younger? Did she concern herself with birth control?

When she was a little girl, I used to talk to her about sex. I didn't want her to be fearful and uptight, as my mother had raised me to be. For a while I waited for her to come to me with questions–"Where do babies come from?" or "Why do you and Daddy like to kiss?" She never did. So I went to her–she must have been about nine or ten–sat her next to me on the chenille bedspread and talked to her about her body, the miracle of sexuality that would one day unfold for her. The poignancy of desire. The electric current of lust. She listened gravely and with patience, as if indulging me, a soft tolerant smile on her lips. I asked if she had any questions. She didn't.

Now I could no more imagine asking her about her erotic life than I could make such an inquiry of a nun or priest. Madrigal's body seemed composed not so much of matter, of blood and sinew, as of light. She'd let her hair grow in; in fact, now she never cut it. When loose it swung below the curve of her buttocks, draping over her narrow shoulders, a tarnished gold, but most of the time she wrapped her head in a peach colored turban. No, not peach, more of a pale orange. Deeper than sherbet; redder than cantaloupe. I never could find the word to describe the color she now dressed in–long pants or skirts that swept the floor. She made a soft glow in whatever room she was standing. I was glad her grandparents were no longer alive to see her. Not that I was ashamed of her, but there would have been no way to make them understand.

On her last trip she was gone longer than she'd ever been before. Twenty-three months. We got postcards from Pakistan, Australia, Jakarta, Japan, India. Josh and I began to think that perhaps Madrigal was gone for good, that this time she would not return to our home. That she had at last found someplace to root. We felt sadness at this prospect, and we felt relief. Not because we didn't like to have her around, but because we wanted her to have a life of her own.

That spring Josh had decided to retire from his law practice. "I want to get back to the things I'm interested in while I'm still young enough to enjoy them," he said, although he was perhaps as vague as I was about exactly what those interests were. We talked about turning Madrigal's room into an office for him. "I could build some bookshelves on that wall," he'd say, "and haul my chair up and put it in that corner." But we could not bring ourselves to paint over the saffron walls, dismantle the altar under the window with its crystals, its candleholders, its brass Buddha.

Then in August, just before her twenty-seventh birthday, Madrigal came home. I'd been out at Costco and arrived back at the house with the car loaded: cases of toilet paper and paper towels, bottled water and soymilk. When I walked in there was an unusual aroma, something I couldn't identify, spicy and murky at the same time, and I called out, "Maddie? Honey? Are you here?" She stepped from her room and came to the top of the stairs. She stood there shyly, as if embarrassed to be seen, and in fact, at first I scarcely recognized her. She wore a gown of pale coral that fell simply from her shoulders to the ground, shiny, like silk. Even with the drape of her dress I could tell she was thin, too thin, and her skin had a pale, yellowed cast to it that clashed with the warm color of her robe. Her face held something else too, but it would be only later, upon reflection, that I would understand it as fear.

I gave no indication of this observation. I set down my shopping bags on the Italian tile and climbed the carpeted stairs to enfold her in a hug. "Welcome home, baby," I said. In my arms I could feel the sharp points of her hipbones, her shoulders. She felt brittle. "You were gone a long time this time," I whispered into her neck. There was a dry smell to her skin, like dust. I held on.

She pulled back to look at me. The green irises of her eyes looked fractured and chipped as granite. "I'm back," she said simply, in a voice more ragged than I'd heard before.

"And with what are you going to be taking over my kitchen this time?" I teased her to cover my distress. "Sprouting some exotic beans you picked up in Marrakech?"

Her lips stretched in the direction of a smile but never quite reached their destination. Instead she ducked her head and said nothing.

"I'm only kidding," I hastened to explain.

"I know."

"All right," I took a step backward. I needed to get my breath. "I've got to unload the car." I hardly knew what to do in the face of her tentativeness, her awkward hesitation. "You put me to shame, Maddie; you live so simply, and I just keep acquiring more stuff."

I started down the stairs but turned back to glance at her again. "Want to come down and talk to me while I put things away?"

I didn't know why I'd said that. Madrigal had always been the most self-contained person I'd ever known, and never seemed to lack for something with which to occupy herself. Even as a little girl she'd never been bored, never come to me complaining about wanting something to do. But standing there in the upstairs hallway, her bony arms poking out the bare sleeves of her dress, she seemed to me strangely adrift, more lost than I'd ever seen her. It broke my heart.

Later that night, after we'd gone upstairs to bed, Josh asked me, "Is she all right?" She'd made only a brief appearance since he'd been home, and I didn't know how much he'd noticed. I'd kept my concerns to myself, wanting the chance to think more clearly about what to do.

"I'm not at all sure she is," I confessed. We both lapsed into a worried silence.

It took me a few days to notice that my daughter wasn't eating. I knew she didn't come to the table to dine with us, but that had long before stopped being a reliable ritual with her. I kept expecting to come across the pulpy discards from her vegetable juice in the garbage disposal, or a pool of black, glossy watermelon seeds in the trash. But not a plate was disturbed except what my husband and I used; not a cup was moved from the cabinet. And I was pretty sure she wasn't eating out either, because as near as I could tell, she hadn't left the house since she'd arrived.

It had been years since I'd made any attempt to question my daughter's habits, eccentric as they might seem to me. I'd always felt that Madrigal was guided by her own Divine light. How could I presume to challenge that, to interfere? But now the glow that had always seemed to radiate from her was faded, its cast cool and dim, and I felt afraid for her.

"I'm going to talk to her," I said to Josh later that night. "I think she might be in trouble." This idea was profoundly unsettling to me. What if we had been wrong about her all these years? What if she'd needed us to be different with her?

"That's a good idea," he agreed. "Do you want me to be there? Or do you think she'll feel like we're ganging up on her?" I saw how he, too, was afraid to transgress our daughter's life.

"I'll do it," I assured him, and watched relief melt into his face.

So I waited until he'd left the next morning for his volunteer shift with Heal the Bay. I watched him back the Volvo out of the drive and disappear down the street, listening as the noise of his engine blended into the buzz of a summer morning. Then I climbed the stairs and knocked on Madrigal's door.

It took a long time for her to answer, and at first I worried that she'd been asleep. I waited a few moments, then knocked again. When at last I heard, "Come in," and turned the knob, I found her sitting upright on a meditation cushion beneath the window with the curtains splayed, sun streaming onto her body.

She was naked, and I could observe more starkly the prominent arch of her ribs, the slackened curve of her breasts, the protruding knobs of her spine. That spine so perfectly erect, her palms open against her knees.

"Maddie…" It was a kind of gasp that escaped me before I knew it would.

She smiled up at me then, and this smile held its old beatific quality. The heat of the sun had lain a fine sheen on her skin, and in the light she once more looked radiant.

Still, I could not ignore the sharp, drawn planes of her face, the shadows under her eyes. I took a deep breath, then plunged. "Honey, I'm concerned. Your Dad and I are… Why aren't you eating?"

Her laughter tinkled out of her, weak but musical. "Because, Mommy…" When was the last time she had called me Mommy? "I don't need to…"

"What are you talking about?" I interrupted her. When was the last time I'd interrupted her? "Of course you need to eat. Without food you'll die!"

She blinked twice; when had I ever been this forceful with her? Then her face broke into its familiar expression of bemused tolerance, a look that ordinarily reassured me, but not now.

"I'm teaching my body to live on light and prana," she told me. "Breath." As if to illustrate, she took a deep inhalation, seeming to savor it with every cell of her being.

A "breatharian," she went on to explain, is similar to a vegetarian, or a fruitarian. But a breatharian doesn't eat vegetables or fruits or anything at all. The breatharian, my daughter insisted, can transmute the energy of light and breath to feed herself.

"That's not possible…" I began, but she continued.

"Yes it is!" she insisted. "It's the highest form of spiritual evolution. There are people who've done it for years."

She must have seen the look on my face because she kept on. "I didn't make this up! There are books about it; you can look it up on the Internet!"

I could feel my temper surging. "That is the craziest thing I ever heard." Before I knew it I was yelling down at my naked daughter. "I've put up with your nutty notions for years—no meat; nothing with a face; nothing with a mother; no, just vegetables; no, just raw foods; juice fasts." Some other voice was rising out of me like a giant hand.

"Look at you," I couldn't stop this voice, this force moving inside me. "You're like a skeleton. Your skin is practically gray; your eyes are dull. Do you expect me to sit here and watch you starve yourself to death in my own house? I need to get you to a hospital!" I was shrieking. I scarcely recognized myself. In twenty-seven years I had never spoken to her this way. If she hadn't been so weak, I would have never done this. It was as if the intensity of my anger provided its own justification.

"No, please don't. It's hard, Mommy," she said then, and I couldn't remember ever seeing her face so naked. It was empty of the certitude I was accustomed to in my daughter, on which I'd come to rely. "I've always felt God wanted me to serve in a special way. It meant I couldn't be like other people." She sounded apologetic. "And I've done whatever I could to open myself, to be a better channel for that Spirit to work through."

My daughter's face was open and full of searching, yet there was courage there too. Commitment. "But this is the hardest test yet. And...I don't know. It takes so much faith. I don't know if I have enough."

She ducked her chin then, and I stared at the top of her head, the dull gold swirl of her hair. When she was a baby, I used to kiss this spot, and I was flooded suddenly with a memory of the sweet powdery scent that used to rise off her infant skin. What did she need from me now? To intervene, take control of her destiny, safeguard her body? Or to give her strength, invest in her the faith she needed to continue on her path?

My anger drained from me in one great rush, and left my knees too jellied to stand. I let my body sink to the rough carpet beside Madrigal, allowing the floor beneath to steady me.

Tears had begun to leak from her eyes; it had been so many years since I'd seen her cry. I opened my arms then, enfolded her slender frame, pulled her into my lap. I sat there for a long time, holding and rocking my daughter, Madrigal, my saint, my mortal child, the sun streaming through the window, flowing over us both.

outside of town

"I'm telling," Jeremy's voice taunted but his eyes popped with fear.

"Go ahead, then." Lisette shrugged, not even turning around to look at him. "Go right on and tell."

She lifted her arm to shoulder height, narrowed her eyes, and once more squeezed the trigger, firing another bullet in the direction of the scarred oak tree. She tried to follow its path with her gaze but it was too fast for her. All she could do was aim and send it on its way; after that the bullet was on its own to seek its destination.

Though it was still early in the morning the sun was already hot in the sky. Lisette rested the pistol in the dirt by her feet, and pulled out a square white handkerchief to wipe her forehead. She lifted the roots of her pale red ponytail and daubed at the back of her neck. The hankie belonged to her father, pulled from a neat pile in the corner of the top drawer of his dresser – the only things in that dresser still in a neat pile, a year after her mother had gone. Lisette had given her father the handkerchiefs a couple of years ago on his birthday. Since he never used them, she figured she might as well.

Lisette turned and watched Jeremy running up to the house. She couldn't imagine who he thought he would tell.

The girl picked up the gun and released the chamber, rolling it open in her palm. Digging around in the pocket of her jeans, she fished out a couple more bullets, dropping them into the empty holes. Then she clicked the chamber back into place and raised her arm again.

She had a good ache in her shoulder where her arm absorbed the impact. She was proud of the way she'd learned to hold herself steady, to keep her eyes open and her arm extended forward as the gun went off.

She lowered her arm back down as she looked around for something to shoot at. She'd shot at the tree, she'd shot at dirt, she'd shot at an old pile of rubber tires leaning against the shed. She didn't want to shoot at anything that was alive – not birds or lizards or snakes.

Lisette sat down in the dirt and stared at the house. She wished that Jeremy would come back but she knew he wouldn't. She pulled out the handkerchief, a little sweat-stained now, and held it up before her face.

With her finger she traced the blue embroidery thread that spelled out JJH. James John Horton, is what that stood for. James John Horton, her father's name. JJ.

It was her father's gun too. One of them. Lisette lay on her back, even though sharp gravel bit into her skin through her thin cotton shirt. She still held the gun, and had an impulse to shoot right straight up into the sky. But the bullet might fall down again and kill her. Or it might shoot an innocent bird who just happened to be flying by.

Lisette closed her eyes and imagined that her mother was there. In this vision her mother had very curly hair piled up on top of her head and Lisette thought she could see some tiny flowers woven in through the curls. Lisette's mother wore a green dress with a wide circle skirt and white high heels and white jewelry. She had a bright red mouth and there was a tall guy in a blue work shirt by her side.

Lisette saw herself pointing the pistol in the direction of the man in the work shirt. "Don't move," she growled to her mother with a sinister leer. "If you move, he gets it." Or maybe she should say to him, "If you try to take her, she gets it." She thought about squeezing the trigger, burning a hole in that blue shirt, or watching a pool of red soak the green dress.

She opened her eyes. She was all sweaty again, a little dizzy from the hot sun. She sat up and noticed Jeremy coming from the house in her direction. He was wearing a white shirt and a pair of navy blue shorts from which his chubby legs descended sockless into sneakers. Jeremy was her cousin, and her aunt Lula sometimes drove him out here to spend the night.

Jeremy only came about halfway from the house to the point where Lisette sat on the ground. He stood there, determined that he'd come close enough, and hollered, "I'm goin' home!"

Lisette used the pistol to shade her eyes from the sun. She saw

Jeremy take a step backwards. "You can't!," she called back. "You got to wait for JJ to come and drive you home."

"No I don't! I called mama to come and get me!"

Lisette considered the probability of this, but she rejected it. She knew from her father that aunt Lula drove Jeremy out here when she had a man friend she wanted to spend the night with. She didn't usually come back until late Sunday, long after JJ had already come home from wherever he went on Saturday night.

She felt mad at Jeremy for being such a baby, so she said, "Liar! You didn't call your mama. Aunt Lula won't even be home 'til t'night."

Jeremy looked like he might be about to cry. "Oh yes I did. My mama's comin' right now and she said I don't ever hafta come back here."

"Okay Jeremy," she yelled. "Bye bye." She swiveled in the dirt and turned her back to him. She could feel him staring at her for a long time, but then after while she turned around and he was gone again.

Jeremy was only eight years old. He wasn't really very good company for Lisette, who was almost eleven, so she didn't really care if he told aunt Lula and never came back again.

According to Jeremy, aunt Lula didn't know that JJ always left them alone on Saturday night, usually right after dinner of hot dogs or macaroni and cheese, and didn't come back till after mid-day Sunday. She didn't know that Lisette and Jeremy stayed up late and made popcorn or fudge or chocolate chip cookies and watched scary movies until the TV went off.

He always said this to Lisette as though she should do something about it – make JJ stay at home or make sure aunt Lula never found out. As far as Lisette could see, aunt Lula didn't really give much of a damn, as long as she had a place to bring Jeremy.

Lisette watched a lizard scurry over the dirt, its skin the same dull brown as the dust it ran across. She stared up at the sun. It shouldn't be long now before JJ came home.

Sometimes there was a woman – never the same one – in the cab of her father's pick-up truck when he came home Sundays. If so then he would disappear into the back of the house with her and not come out again for a couple of hours. Lisette never went out of her way to meet these women. But if he came back by himself sometimes he brought along a bucket of fried chicken and some mashed potatoes and biscuits from the take-out place in town, and then she and Jeremy and JJ would all sit at the kitchen table together and eat and watch sports on TV.

She sat there, not thinking about very much at all, when she was surprised to see aunt Lula's old white convertible raising a cloud of dust as it pulled into the driveway. Lisette scrambled up and secreted herself behind the oak tree. The woman got out of the car but made no move to walk up the driveway or into the house. Instead she pulled out a cigarette and lit it.

Lisette watched Jeremy come out of the house with his knapsack. She could read her aunt's irritation in the set of her shoulders, in the short jabbing motions she made to smoke her cigarette, in the way she gestured to Jeremy to get in the car. Jeremy pulled open the heavy door and started to climb in, but then he turned and looked toward the oak tree. He hopped back out of the car and ran toward the tree, glancing over his shoulder at his mother to indicate that she wait a minute.

Lisette watched him come stumbling over the weedy grass, stopping again at the same distance he had before. She wasn't about to come out from behind the tree, and Jeremy seemed to know that. Still he called out to her as though they were staring each other right in the eye.

"I came to say good-bye!," he yelled at the tree. Jeremy stared intently at the rough bark, as if trying to decipher a response. He reached down sideways to scratch a mosquito bite on his leg. "I don't think she'll let me come back here anymore."

From behind Jeremy, his mother began honking the horn. What he had to say must be important to keep her waiting, but he seemed unsure of how to do it. He stared at the silhouette of white where Lisette's shirt was visible against the edge of the tree trunk.

Finally he blurted, "Don't shoot yourself, Lisette!" Then the boy turned and ran as fast as he could back to the car.

Lisette could see aunt Lula behind the wheel again, revving the engine and almost driving off as Jeremy reached the car door, just to let him know how impatient she was with this whole thing. Then Lisette watched as the tailfins disappeared down the long ribbon of highway that led back to town.

She waited until she could no longer see the car, then she counted to 350 after that before she came out from behind the oak. Jeremy was nothin' but a damn baby. She was pretty sure he wouldn't be coming back out here again, but she was also pretty sure she wasn't going to get in any trouble for it either.

Lisette craned her neck and looked up at the sky, right into the face of the sun. She guessed JJ was late today. Then she chuckled to herself. JJ was late and aunt Lula was early. Wonder what that could mean?

She was tired of being outdoors but she didn't really want to go in either. She had made pancakes for herself and Jeremy this morning and there was stuff to clean up, but she knew it would just make her sad.

Lisette looked at the pistol she'd been holding all this time. Jeremy was just stupid, that's all. Why would she want to do something like that? She thought about what it would be like to shoot at one of aunt Lula's tailfins as she made her getaway with Jeremy.

She looked out across the brown field toward the road. Waves of heat rose from the blacktop, interrupted only by the passing of an occasional car. Each time, it wasn't JJ. Lisette felt hot and tired and bored.

Then she got an idea. Lisette reached back into her pocket and pulled out the crumpled white handkerchief. She walked over to the oak tree and tied the cloth to some low branches. She spread it out to its full size, like a tiny sail, except there was no wind at all.

She backed away and studied the cloth. Went back to the tree and retied one corner of it. Stepped back and studied it again.

Cheerful now, full of purpose, she turned and walked ten paces, carefully measuring each one with the length of a footfall, no more, no less. When she'd achieved her distance she turned and raised her right arm.

Her gaze traveled down the length of her arm to the nose of the gun, then beyond that silver gateway through the hot air until it rested on the square of white cloth. Her eyes squinted until they focused on the blue threads that looped ornately through the handkerchief.

Without blinking, Lisette fired.

twentynine palms

The clock by the bed read ten-thirty when Tina awoke with a throbbing head and a queasy stomach. It took her a minute to bring her eyes into focus in the dark room. All the shades were pulled down against the sun, which pushed into the window, merciless.

Jesus, it was already a hundred degrees. She tried to gather the will to rise. Tina dimly noticed that she was still in her clothes from yesterday, that her mouth felt dry and sour.

With great care she disentangled herself from the sheet and swung one leg experimentally over the side of the bed to rest on the floor. Swinging the other leg required her to sit up, which made her dizzy. She groped by the side of the bed for a cigarette, lit one, inhaled. She was sweating.

Goddamn Ned, dragging her out to live in this goddamn desert in this shitbox house with no air conditioning. She stared bitterly around the room, which was littered with piles of discarded clothes, underwear, socks. Leaving her cigarette on the edge of the night table, Tina hoisted herself into a standing position, grabbing onto the dresser as she waited for the room to stop spinning. Then she shuffled through the door.

The tiny tiled bathroom smelled awful, and she noticed a stream of vomit in the bathtub. It was pale red. She had been drinking Tequila Sunrises last night, and at the memory her stomach threatened to turn over again. Where had she been? Tina strained to remember. Oh yeah, she and Ned were home last night. She tried to form a picture of Ned sleeping next to her in the bed, but the screen stayed blank.

Trying not to focus on what she was doing, Tina ran the shower to wash away the orangey-pink in the tub. She stripped off her stale and slightly sticky clothes and left them in a heap on the floor. As the vomit swirled down the drain, she stepped in and under the spray, which was scalding. Moving faster than she could have predicted, Tina hopped out again and turned on the cold tap, then gingerly stepped back in.

She let the warm water stream over her back, wet but did not wash her hair. Climbing out of the shower, Tina grabbed a towel, which she wiped half-heartedly over her skin, then discarded. At the sink she spread a thick slab of Gleem on her toothbrush and stuck it in her mouth, sloshing the suds around inside to neutralize the sour taste. She dropped the toothbrush into the sink and walked naked toward the kitchen. Already she was sweating again.

The front rooms were streaming with light, which intensified the pain thudding over her eyes. She closed drapes and blinds until the room dimmed. In the kitchen she pulled instant coffee down from the shelf and spooned a big heap into the bottom of a cup. With one hand she turned the gas on under the kettle while at the same time reaching to open the refrigerator door. The momentary rush of cool air was reviving. Grabbing a carton of orange juice, she took a big swig, then shuddered as the citrus crazed against the mint taste of toothpaste. She plucked a glass from the dish drainer, sloshed some juice into it, and left the carton on the countertop. Just as the kettle started to scream she pulled it off the range and poured hot water over the coffee powder. She gulped some immediately, which burned her tongue, then dropped back onto a plastic-covered folding chair, defeated.

Christ, she had to get this place cleaned up. She looked at the mess of glasses and half-empty cans that cluttered the kitchen. A big spill on the floor hadn't been wiped up. Ashtrays exploded with cigarette butts. Goddamn it.

She wandered back into the bedroom and noticed that her cigarette had dropped ashes onto the carpet and burned a wedge in the top of the night table. She opened a drawer and fished out a pair of running shorts, which had fit her before she put on ten pounds. To this she added a halter top she had owned since she was eighteen. It would do for around the house.

She forced herself to return to the kitchen, where she began stacking glasses in the sink, throwing garbage and aluminum cans into a paper bag. She'd get everything straightened up and then she'd feel better. Coffee was bringing her back but her head still pounded and the heat was doing nothing to help.

Tina reached into the freezer and popped a couple of ice cubes into her juice. Before closing it she stuck her face into the tiny area, deeply inhaling the frosty air. Then she tipped the big bottle of vodka on the kitchen table and poured some into her glass. Just for her head, she promised. This made her feel much better and she felt her energy pick up just a little.

She even turned on the portable radio to the rock 'n roll station, though she kept it low. Rock 'n roll wasn't like how it was when she was in high school. All this heavy metal. High school seemed like a long time ago, but she still remembered it. She'd be thirty-five her next birthday; she didn't want to think about that.

Tina had been cocktail waitressing in a little place in San Bernardino when she'd met Ned. In this bar she'd worn a little costume, a short black skirt and a ruffled pink shirt, cut low, black nylons and high heels. The outfit had made her feel glamorous. Ned was not a regular. Said he'd just stopped in on his way home. Home was in Twentynine Palms and he had the bluest eyes beaming out of darkly tanned skin. Ned had joked with her and she'd teased back, flirting a little. When he asked her to go home with him after the bar closed she'd said okay and followed his pick-up through the dark in her banged-up Ford wagon.

The sex was great and she'd stayed around for a couple of days, calling into work with "cramps." When he suggested she quit her job and move in with him she surprised him by saying okay again. She'd hoped to work on her tan. She was tired of the bar. She thought it would be glamorous to live so near to Palm Springs. That was sixteen months ago.

Ned had a job with a construction company that built new condos in the desert, of which there never seemed to be too many. He left early in the morning, often before Tina awakened, and came home late, tired, dirty. He made good money, but his child support payments ate up a lot of it. Sometimes on weekends they would have Ned's two boys over. She always felt like an outsider around them, and god knows she didn't have the energy for touch football. Even feeding them was a pain, especially the oldest, who always went out of his way to tell her that his mom cooked it better.

In those sixteen months, Tina had decided that Twentynine Palms was a lot like San Bernardino, only smaller and more boring. And Palm Springs! Half the year the town was crowded with tourists from L.A., decked out in white clothes and expensive cars, people who looked through her on the street. The rest of the year it was empty and dead.

She didn't like the desert either. It was hot, flat, boring. The light was always too bright. It was always windy at night, and everything got so dusty. It just wasn't for her. Maybe if she had a swimming pool or something. She used to like to get a tan when she was younger. But now it seemed stupid and boring to lay around in the sun; she could only sit still for five minutes at a time. She didn't want to get skin cancer either.

By about one-thirty the kitchen was cleaned up, and Tina had had three glasses of vodka and juice. It was too hot; she didn't have it in her to do any more housework.

She pulled some ground beef out of the freezer and left it in the sink to defrost. She'd try and cook something for Ned tonight. He got pissed off when he came home and the place wasn't picked up and his supper wasn't on the table. He just didn't know what it was like there during the day.

Now Tina remembered a little about the night before. Ned was pissed because she hadn't cooked dinner, even though she'd had a batch of Tequila Sunrises all blended up, chilled and waiting for him. She couldn't remember the fight, but she guessed he'd left and not come home. Probably spent the night with one of his buddies from the crew.

She was out of orange juice now but she reached for some more ice and poured the clear vodka over it. Just had to do something to keep cool on a day like this. She intended to clean up the rest of the house, but Jesus, it was the hottest part of the day.

They just had to get an air conditioner. She lay down on the couch in the living room and set the glass on her bare belly. She pulled an ice cube out of the glass, sucked the vodka off of it, and placed it on her forehead to melt. It felt good. Little drops ran down her temples and into her hair. She closed her eyes and tried to remember something good.

Tina thought about Ned. He used to call her during the day from the site but not anymore. She tried to remember the last time they had sex but she couldn't focus on that. Then she thought back to their anniversary. Even though they never got married they still celebrated their anniversary. She had tried to fix something special, some Greek chicken dish out of Redbook. But the chicken didn't turn out, and Ned got home really late, and the pitcher of martinis had gotten watery, and they'd had a fight.

She skipped over thinking about Carl, who she had married at twenty and divorced at twenty-six. Carl had always told her she was stupid, but she wasn't stupid enough to spend the rest of her life with him. She thought back to her high school prom and about the guys she'd dated in high school, then all the way back to the time when she was growing up in Fontana. But nothing seemed good, at least not good enough to remember.

Tears welled up in the corners of her eyes and she sobbed a little. After she stopped crying she got up and put more ice cubes in her glass and poured the rest of the vodka.

She lay on the couch again, placing her glass against her temples, her chest, the insides of her wrists, trying to cool down. Tina didn't think about anything at all, just pressed the icy glass up and down her body, intermittently sipping from it, until the ice had melted and the glass was drained.

She lay there for a while, feeling the heat press around her from every direction. In three more minutes she was going to get up and go clean that bathroom, and at least make the bed. She rolled over onto her side, curling under her cheek the rough upholstered cushion.

Tina then became aware that the radio was still playing, and she recognized a song that had been popular in high school. "Gotta keep those lovin' good vibrations happenin' with her," the Beach Boys sang. She could remember that song from a particular night when she'd gone out to a carnival with some boy. James or Joe, something like that. He had won her a big stuffed beagle in a shooting game. Riding home in his car, she had cuddled up against his side, holding the big plush dog in her arms. That song on the radio. The night all around them. She thought she remembered that they'd kissed. She'd never gone out with him again though. She didn't know why.

Tina lurched up then. The room spun around a little, then righted itself as she went back to the kitchen. The vodka was empty. The sight of the empty bottle surprised her. She unscrewed the top and stared one-eyed down to its clear bottom. She inhaled over the lip. Squinting at the clock she saw that it was almost five. She could be out and back before Ned got home.

Picking up speed she went into the bedroom and stuffed her feet into an old pair of backless platform shoes, the wooden heels nicked and scarred. Then she grabbed her change purse and car keys off the dresser and left the house.

Outside it was still scorching but the winds had picked up, blowing grit that stuck to her skin. She climbed into the old blue wagon, the only thing she still had from her marriage to Carl. She slammed the door, ground the key into the ignition. The engine sputtered but did not catch. She tried again, pushing the accelerator to the floor and holding it there. In the back of her mind she heard Ned, pump it, don't floor it, you'll flood it. This time the engine turned over, and Tina threw it victoriously into gear. She screeched out of her driveway, followed the road that wound her out of her tract, and pulled out onto the main highway.

Sweat was gathering underneath her breasts. All the windows were down and the hot desert wind blew through the car as she sped down the road that led toward Palm Springs. She liked to go all the way into town to buy her liquor, she liked the store where there were shelves and shelves of bottles full of colored liquid. It was good for her to get out of the house too. Ned was always telling her that.

As she drove she began to plan the supper she would fix that night. She rehearsed each step: unwrapping the hamburger from its white paper, the soggy feel of the pink meat in her hands. Pulling out a couple of slices of white bread and tearing them into small spongy morsels, then soaking them in a bowl of milk. Finally mixing the soaked bread together with the ground meat and slapping them into patties. That was a recipe she had learned in high school, in Home Ec. She was pretty sure they still had some of that potato salad she'd gotten at the market last week, and she could boil up a pouch of frozen green beans.

Tina nearly collided with a Blazer as she pulled out from behind a car full of Mexicans doing thirty miles an hour. A horn blast caught her attention and she moved back across the double line just in time to avoid being hit head-on. She applied a little more pressure to the accelerator. She would have to get home soon so she could have everything ready for Ned when he walked in.

Finally she pulled up alongside the Liquor Barn and stopped the car. She sat still for a moment, trying to absorb the fact of her arrival. Her vision was blurry and she felt sleepy in the hot car.

Slowly she shoved open the car door. It seemed very heavy and she was furious when it swung back to close again. The second time Tina plunked both feet down on the pavement, then maneuvered herself out from behind the steering wheel. She felt unsteady on her wooden heels and swayed slightly, standing in the parking lot. Then she realized she had left her change purse in the car. Closing one eye, she aimed the key at the lock. After several passes she got the car open again and leaned over to pick up the pink plastic pouch from the passenger seat. Coming up, she cracked her head on the edge of the door and nearly dropped to her knees in pain. She leaned against the searing roof of the car, head down on her arms, until she regained her balance.

Finally she straightened and got herself into the store. A rush of unnaturally cold air hit her as she entered though the automatic doors and gooseflesh stood up all over her body. But the cold air was a relief after sweating all day. She might just stay here all night.

But then Tina began to worry about the time. She really wanted to be there when Ned got home. She didn't know what he'd think if she wasn't. She should have left him a note. Tina didn't take her usual time to browse among the shelves of bottles, letting her eyes ramble over the variations of shapes and colors. Instead she picked up a big half-gallon of vodka, a fifth of tequila and a fifth of scotch, Ned's favorite. As an after-thought she added a cold six-pack to her cart and went to the check-out.

The cashier eyed her for a moment, seemed to be about to say something. Tina briefly panicked, thinking she might be asked to show her i.d. and where was her driver's license? But the clerk thought better of it, only uttered the total of what she owed. Tina opened her coin purse, unrolled a stack of bills and painstakingly counted out the right amount. Then she dropped the purse, spilling coins across the shiny linoleum. She stooped to retrieve them, but felt so dizzy that she only scooped up the pink bag and stood again slowly, leaving the dimes, quarters, and pennies where they lay.

She grabbed the brown paper sack and, tightly clutching her purse and the remaining bills, she walked out, keeping her head up and her eyes straight ahead. The outdoor air blasted her, but she just kept walking to her car, opened it up, set her bag on the passenger seat, and collapsed behind the steering wheel.

Tears came then, and Tina rested her head on the wheel until they passed. Then she started the old car, and impulsively reached inside the bag for a can of beer. She popped it open and took a long drink before she put the wagon in gear and drove back out onto the highway.

The cold beer helped her to focus her concentration as she pressed the accelerator. She felt a little panicky now about the time. She hadn't worn a watch in years, and she tried to imagine what time it could be. The sun went down about eight-thirty these days, she thought, and from a glance in the rear-view mirror, it looked like it had a while to go. But she couldn't remember exactly when she'd left the house, nor how long this drive was supposed to take. Ned usually got home about six-thirty. Could it be six-thirty yet?

The beer can was sweating in her hand. She set it on the seat beside her and reached over to turn on the radio, even though it had been getting only one station – a station that broadcast in Spanish – ever since she'd moved to Twentynine Palms. Tina didn't habla español, not since high school. As she heard the familiar Latin beat and the incomprehensible lyrics, she snapped the radio off in disgust.

She began to drive even faster. The speedometer crept past sixty. Tumbleweeds and trailer parks flashed by in a blur. She thought about stopping somewhere to call him but she kept driving.

Oh shit and the house was such a mess. She never had finished cleaning. Ned would be mad about that and... As she drove, Tina began to watch a movie in her mind. Last night. She had been taking a nap on the couch when Ned got in, and she had already sampled the Tequila Sunrises that were blended up in a pitcher in the refrigerator as a surprise for Ned. He had come in, very sunburnt and crusted with dirt. Then he had started yelling about how the house was a mess and there was no dinner ready and how did she think it felt to go out and do construction work every day and come home to a slut in a pig-sty. Tina had just lain there, squinting up at him, trying to shake the heaviness from her brain and waiting for him to cool down. Then she had offered him a drink.

Tina saw a picture of Ned, grabbing the pitcher from the refrigerator, her getting up to get glasses, him raising the pitcher and tilting it. She could almost feel again the sweet sticky redness pouring over her, dripping from her hair, stinging her eyes, the sharp sour smell of tequila all over her. Then she was on the floor, sitting in her own puddle. She heard her own voice crying and promising she wouldn't drink anymore. And Ned was crying too as he slammed out the door.

Tina almost missed the turnoff for her block, but she yanked the wheel and squealed onto the smaller road just in time. She raced down it, taking the curves as dust flew up and into the windows. Finally her street, and then the little tract house. Ned's truck was not in the driveway.

Tina turned off the engine and sat still, listening to the wind and the other sounds of evening gathering around her. She sat there for a long time, long after the sun went down and it was night in the desert.

news

"The ship is reported to contain over five hundred children, some of them as young as three years old, destined for the slave trade in Benin." Before my eyes the newsprint blurs and I feel the hot splash of tears on my cheeks. I close my eyes and I am a child, just three, snatched from my parents or maybe I've had no parents, and I am in the hold of the ship, packed in with so many others. The smell of sweat and excrement and vomit. The endless motion of the sea. Am I afraid or is it all too awful to be able to feel even that? And what awaits me even worse...

"Jesus Christ, Tracy." Dani stares at me from the kitchen door, her face a collage of pity and disgust. She's just finished forty-five minutes on the treadmill; her face is flushed. A tornado of sweat swirls between her breasts, staining her tee shirt. She's taken in the tears that streak my face, my white knuckles gripping my coffee mug.

"What is it this time? The Palestinians? The earthquake victims?"

"It's the year 2001 and children are being sold into slavery..." I begin, but she waves away my words, barely disguising her irritation. She comes around behind my chair, wraps her arms around my neck. She smells salty and unfresh.

"Honey, stop reading the damn paper if it makes you so upset."

I twist out of her grasp so I can glare at her. "Everything that's going on in this world, and you think the answer is to just stop reading?"

I know the look she's giving me, the look that signals "All the lesbians in L.A. and I had to get stuck with the one who's too sensitive to live."

"I don't see it doing much good to sit here and cry about it. Life isn't that bad," she rationalizes.

I stand now, to equalize the height advantage. "Dani, that's just the attitude that makes me crazy! I can't just pretend that life is great and everything's fine when there's suffering going on all over the world!" I sweep my hand across the front page to illustrate my point.

"Okay, but what about the suffering going on in your own house? I mean it, Tracy, you're driving me nuts with this stuff. Work is hard enough. I just want to get up on a Saturday morning and have breakfast without having to take on all the world's problems before noon! I'm about ready to cancel the subscription."

"Excuse me? I pay for the paper." I'm not backing down on this.

"Christ, baby, when was the last time you laughed? Or told a joke? Yeah, all right, the world's a mess–what else is new? But face it, there's not a damn thing you or I can do about it."

I don't agree. Doesn't human misery deserve at least a witness? But I'll never convince Dani of that. She doesn't want to probe too deep or feel too much. Things are exactly as they seem for Dani. On her birthday, she celebrates. On the weekend, she relaxes. She goes to work and does her job and never questions if this is what she should be doing with her life.

I look at her, her short gold hair disheveled from sleep, sweat-plastered to her head. The way she looks so cute in her exercise shorts and tee shirt. We've been together three years. I love her, or at least I think I do. But staring at her now, she's the one who seems grainy as newsprint, composed of atoms like ink dots; it's those floating children who seem real to me, compelling.

"Hey," I say, folding up the paper to carry to the recycling bin. It's a conciliatory gesture. "Want to go check out that antique place Tanya was telling me about?"

Her face brightens. She's relieved the storm has passed. "Just let me go take a shower." She kisses me before she vanishes down the hall, not just a peck, but slow and sweet.

I try to stay in that moment of her, savoring that kiss, but as I hear water stream into the shower, I spread open the newsprint once more. I try to figure out where this elusive ship with its precious chattel might be hiding. The article contains a quote, some Admiral, "The Navy tried to keep its pursuit a secret. Sometimes, to avoid prosecution, the crew is instructed to just dump its cargo into the sea." Its cargo. I imagine tiny bodies floating in the ocean, splayed angels drifting through layers of blue, strange fish so far from home.

O

Monday morning, and the freeway its own clotted sea. My Honda has moved about three feet in the last fifteen minutes, and the dashboard clock leaves no doubt that I will be late for work. Again.

"…UN investigators uncovered scores of mass graves, each containing the decomposed bodies of dozens of ethnic Albanians…"

Behind my eyelids, the sky is gray, trees leafless, the ground a dead, frozen brown. The air is still bitter, revealing no trace of spring. This land was once farmland, but now the furrows erupt in gaping holes from which sprout a clatter of twisted bones.

A horn blast shocks me back to the freeway, the driver behind me mouthing angry words. I press the accelerator, move forward ten feet. Big deal. I try to remember whether I have any deadlines this morning; I don't think so. I work for a special effects house, and depending on what's due, it's either frantic or slow. This morning I'm hoping for slow.

The story of Srebrenica makes me angry. Ethnic cleansing, it's like Hitler. The Jews promised "Never again," but now the world sits by while what was once Yugoslavia consumes itself. Dani thinks the anger is a waste of energy, but if this doesn't make you angry, what does it take?

My parents always said I was too sensitive. They tell me I used to watch the news on TV when I was a child and cry at the footage of civil rights marchers in Birmingham, chaos on the streets of Saigon, Watt and Detroit and Newark burning. I could feel it as if I was there, the blast of water cannons, the wind whipped by the chopper blades, the hiss and crackle of flame. I never understood how they could behave as if this were all happening to someone else, something for them merely to watch. Couldn't they smell the napalm? They told me I needed to grow a thicker skin.

Sometimes I think my derma is thick and thin in the wrong places. When I was in college, I volunteered at a homeless shelter. Some days I'd work in their kitchen, chopping an endless mound of cabbage or peeling mountains of potatoes. Other days they'd have me sort out the old clothes that people had donated, ragged sweaters and barely worn dress shirts, jeans and trousers and topcoats. I'd hand these out to men with scabs on their faces, men with trembling hands, men who looked at me and did not know who I was. One on one, I felt nothing for them. I'd hand a man a scarf, but I wouldn't care if he were warm tonight or not; usually he smelled bad and I wanted him to go away quickly. I couldn't force my lips into a smile for him, some human fire on which to warm himself.

It was only later, when I'd walk to the bus stop through the streets of downtown L.A., sidewalks lined with cardboard pallets where men and women made their beds for the night. I'd walk for blocks past these cardboard condos and then sometimes I could feel it, the deep sorrow of it all, that thread that connects us.

The news haunts me like a shadow on an X-ray – the latest toxic spill, victims of torture, the decimation of AIDS. Newspaper, television, radio, internet, news enters my body like an IV drip. It seeps into my dreams. How can I turn away?

○

When I met Dani she was working for an organization that delivers food to people with AIDS. It was the first thing she told me about herself, and I loved her instantly for it. She used to come home and tell me about the people on her route: "Alan's parents came to visit; JJ got into a clinical trial; Ricky D went into hospice." I could feel the sharp rattle of pneumocystis in my lungs, my anus raw from the diarrhea of wasting syndrome. I knew the ups and downs of their health. Sometimes we went to their memorials. Then about a year and a half ago she came home and told me she'd quit; she was burned out.

Now Dani sells computer supplies over the telephone; she's good at it, earns big commissions. Last Christmas she took me on a trip to Kona with her year-end bonus.

For weeks Dani's been telling me about Gina; she's so excited that there's another lesbian at her job. Gina plays racquetball. Gina told off the supervisor who questioned her late arrival. Gina and her lover Natalie are having a baby. Their second.

So tonight is the night when I'm finally going to meet Gina and Natalie. A double date. It's taken a few weeks to arrange it because it's hard for them to find a sitter.

I don't want to go. Dani's let go of a lot of the friends she had when she used to work for Project Angel Food and there's something about her descriptions of Gina and Natalie that make my stomach clench. I imagine my evening filled with stories of teething and spit-up; parents are entirely solipsistic and lesbian parents are the worst of all, as if they're over-compensating, as if they have something to prove. I've known since I was a little girl that I didn't want to have children. The lesbian baby boom going on all around me makes me cranky. But here it is, Saturday night, and Dani has made it clear that this is really important to her.

I'm online reading about the Taliban in Afghanistan, the movement's total suppression of women who are no longer allowed to walk on the streets unaccompanied, are forbidden to be educated, and who may be stoned to death for violating any provision of the strict Islamic code. Inside my skull I see the shapes of women covered head to foot in the chador, feel its suffocating heat in the dusty streets of Kabul. I cannot be on this street unless I am accompanied by a husband, a father, or brother.

"Tracy, what are you doing? We're supposed to meet at the restaurant at 7:15."

I shake myself back to the present, bookmark the page before signing off the Internet, shutting down the computer.

"I'm all ready, Dani," I call back. "In fact, I've been waiting for you."

As I come down the hall she looks at me; disappointment flickers across her face. "Is that what you're wearing?"

I look down at myself. I have on a short black dress that is, admittedly, wrinkled from being balled on the floor of my closet overnight, tights with only a couple of runs and black lace-up Doc Maarten boots. Dani said, "Dress up," so I'm wearing what I wore yesterday to work.

I notice that Dani's version of dressed up includes tailored black slacks, a black linen shirt, boots with a heel. Her wardrobe has begun to change since she's been in sales.

Even before she says anything more, I start to argue. "Dani, I thought Natalie was supposed to be pregnant. How glamorous do you think she's going to look?"

"I was just hoping…" she begins, then breaks off, as if giving up. Then tries again. "Maybe you could put your hair up or something."

"Give me a minute." I sulk into the bathroom and stare at myself in the mirror. My face without make-up, the hazel eyes wide, the broad brow. I grab handfuls of my dark brown curly hair, now lightly threaded with silver, pile it on top of my head, and fasten it in place with a jumble of clips. I've seen the young production artists at work pull off this look. I have to admit I look fancier. I go a step further and outline my lips in a dark purple lipstick that accentuates the pallor of my skin.

I pull the black dress over my head, leave it strewn across the towel rack. I go to my closet and pull out a purple velvet dress my mother bought me a few birthdays back. Not something I'd have picked out for myself, but Dani's face lights up when she sees me. "Thanks, baby," she breathes into my neck with a swift kiss. She dares not comment on the tights and boots, which I've retained.

When we arrive at the restaurant and greet our dinner companions, I am chagrined to see that despite her seven-month pregnancy, Natalie is glamorous indeed. She's wearing a loose black dress with a low-cut neckline that reveals her swelling cleavage, and a stylish pair of platform shoes. Gina is garbed in an expensive suit, its trousers knife-pleated, the jacket cut to accentuate her waist. Natalie's blonde hair is salon-cut, her make-up professional, and her nails are manicured. She hangs off Gina's arm like a precious jewel as Dani makes awkward introductions. Within thirty seconds I can tell that I have nothing to say to these women. They are from the planet of the Upbeat.

The restaurant is dark and decorated in a spare aesthetic that signals expensive. One hundred candles glitter around the room. The maitre'd is thin and formal, his face bisected geometrically by a triangle of goatee. As he shows us to our table, Dani keeps her arm around my waist in a way I've never liked, a proprietary gesture that makes me feel like an appendage. I quickly pull out my own chair and sit before she can do it for me.

Gina and Natalie do it properly. Gina pulls out the chair to my right and her partner glides into it, their movements seamless as Gina guides the chair back toward the table, then bends to kiss her lover's ear before seating herself across from me. Dani has plopped down disconsolately to my left.

Gina bends over to whisper something to Natalie; Dani and I sit bolt upright in our chairs, not looking at each other. I pick up the menu for something to do; Dani notices the small frown at the corner of my mouth and scowls.

The waiter appears and introduces himself as "Jake." He is model-handsome with a tanning booth glow to his complexion. He asks for our drink order: sour apple martini for Gina, grapefruit juice for Natalie–she requests, "fresh squeezed"–a Corona for Dani. Jake's eyes turn to me.

"Just water," I say.

"Pellegrino or Evian," he persists.

The whole "status beverage" thing offends me. There are villages in Africa where women must walk several miles for a bucket of sludgy, bacteria-infested water and carry it back across the desert on their head. "Tap," I reply. Dani winces. Jake lifts one eyebrow and disappears.

"Don't you worry about all the stuff they put in the water?" Natalie asks me. Gina and Dani are deep in conversation about printer cartridges, so Natalie and I are left to find something to talk about.

"I do," is all I say. I could tell her about lead and mercury, lindane and atrazine and asbestos, about Cryptosporidium and Giardia, the biological contaminants. I could tell her about trace elements, parts per billion, sources of contamination. I could tell her about rates of infection, the mutation of amphibious creatures, the occurrence of cancer. Gazing at her French manicure, white moons at the tip of each fingernail, I am pretty sure she doesn't want to hear it.

"So when is your due date?" I ask, and am immediately sorry. This is reflexive, the kind of thing one is supposed to say to a pregnant woman; I hear the secretaries in my office make this kind of inquiry. In truth, I'm not the least bit interested in her pregnancy, but I can't imagine what else to say to her.

"I've got eight more weeks to go." Her grin is self-satisfied, smugly content, and I feel a stab of active dislike for her.

She waits; clearly I am expected to ask more questions: Method of insemination? How long did it take? What was it like the first time? How old is your first child? I can see the words clustering just behind her lips, her story, so well polished, ready to pour forth.

But I don't take my cue. Instead, I nod and rearrange my silverware and stare into the dark space of the restaurant. I sip my ice water. It's rude, I suppose, but then, she's not asking me anything either.

Jake reappears and offers temporary distraction. Gina and Dani each order steak–prime rib rare and porterhouse, medium, respectively.

I hate it when Dani eats meat; I can smell it on her skin for days.

Natalie says, "I'd like the scallops, but could you ask the chef to use olive oil instead of butter?" As if she were an old friend for whom there's nothing he wouldn't do, Jake assures her that he will.

He is far less amenable to my own request for a vegetable plate. It's not on the menu, and maybe he thinks it doesn't cost enough. He impatiently scribbles something on his pad, asks, "Will that be all?"

For just a moment, Dani shoots me an accusatory look. Then she says, for the benefit of the table, "Tracy's a vegetarian," as if my order somehow demanded an explanation.

Gina looks astonished, then suspicious. "How do you get your protein?"

I shrug. It's the year 2001; a vegetarian diet is not a radical concept. "The amount of land and crops used to raise cows could feed hundreds of thousands of people…" I begin, but Dani heads me off at the pass.

"Tracy's a really great cook," she says, as if this somehow makes up for my other eccentricities. I narrow my eyes at her.

"So, Tracy, Dani…" Gina wraps an arm around Natalie's shoulders. "Have you given any thought to starting a family?"

"In a few years I think we might…" Dani begins, when I override her with a harsh, "NO."

Natalie chuckles. Our disagreement hangs in the chilled air, turning the moment awkward, which Natalie seems to enjoy. "Sounds like you two have something to discuss," she taunts.

Fuck you, I want to say, but I let my eyes do it for me.

Dani wants to redeem the moment. "We just need to work it through," she says. My jaw drops, I can't believe what I've just heard. I stare at her, stunned by this betrayal. Does she imagine that she can just dismiss my feelings about this?

Then all of a sudden I understand, this thing I've been sensing but haven't been able to grasp until just this minute: This is who Dani wants to be now, who she wants us to be. Like Gina and Natalie. It's like an earthquake; only a few seconds pass, but nothing in my world is left intact. My first impulse is to strike back.

"Actually," I correct her, "I personally believe it's immoral for people to bring more kids into the world, when the planet is so overpopulated we can't feed or care for the ones who are already alive."

All three stare at me, offended, shocked. Dani looks as if she's never seen me before in her life, as Gina angrily protests, "Who are you to judge us?"

Natalie fires off, "You must be a very unhappy woman."

Servers arrive with our order, set the platters before us, and it seems like a good opportunity for a time out. I stand, letting the napkin fall from my lap. "Excuse me," I say, "I need to use the restroom."

I don't know where I'm going so I wander toward the back. I don't find the restroom but I stumble upon the bar, where my eye is caught by the TV, tuned to CNN. I take a seat. The story being reported is about an oil spill off the coast of South America. Volunteers hold blackened birds in their hands, feathers oil-soaked. The bird's heart hammers against human fingers. The waters churn black. The beaches full of dead fish. The fisherman, his eyes already old, gestures toward his now useless boat, his futile nets. If the sea is poisoned, the whole village will starve.

"What the hell happened to you?" Dani's voice is harsh in my ear.

I turn to look at her and for a moment can't figure out why she's angry.

"We're supposed to be out for dinner with my friends," she reads the indictment. "First you insult them, and then you leave to watch TV?"

"I just got caught up in this story about…"

She doesn't let me finish. "What is the matter with you? So some fish die halfway around the world, but you're here!" Her thumb and middle finger snap furiously in front of my face. "Wake up, Tracy. This is your fucking life!"

"You used to care about the world, too," I protest.

She doesn't respond. She turns and strides away, her boot heels clicking on the Italian tile. My eyes wander back to the television, but there's another story now, something about the economic trends of the European Community and I'm not interested. I pay the bartender for the club soda I don't remember ordering. For a moment I consider calling a cab and just going home.

I have no idea how long I've been gone from the table. The bus boy is clearing the table when I return to my seat. My vegetable plate remains untouched.

Gina and Natalie glance at me as I sit, then slide their eyes away. Even if I wanted to, there's no way to salvage the evening. A bloated energy hangs over our table, imposes a thick jagged silence. Jake appears and I ask for my vegetable plate to go. No one wants dessert or coffee.

Outside, Dani says, "We're around the corner." I'm grateful that I persuaded her to look for a parking place on the street, because it means we don't have to wait with our dinner companions for the valet. Our good-byes are hollow and quick. I feel like running down the street back to the car.

Then I am in the passenger seat of Dani's Jeep and the silence is different now, as if night has shrouded us. She's too mad at me to talk, the space between us bruised, swollen, and really, what could I say to her?

So I sit in my seat and lean my forehead against the window; it's cool and hard on my skin. I watch the streetlights pass, one after another. History is a current, I think. I heard that somewhere. I try to imagine myself as part of that flow, that tide. Those who can't see this will be left behind.

Before Dani, I was with a woman named Arshille, a folksinger who played mournful love songs on her twelve-string guitar. She used to sing to me while I read the newspaper. When she left, she told me I was cold, that my preoccupation with world events was my shield against a personal life. "You're going to end up alone, Tracy," she warned, "with nothing but your newspapers for comfort." I missed the smell of jasmine that always surrounded her, missed the long red hair that she would sweep across my belly when we made love.

For a while after that, I stopped looking at the news, started meditating instead, going each morning to the Zen Center to sit on a cushion on the floor and quiet my thoughts. When it was best I could slip inside a kind of emptiness, like a pocket, held within its soft folds, my whole mind white. I could feel myself and my connection to everyone else inside that silky blankness. That's what I was doing when I met Dani.

Dani always says she fell in love with me because she saw me dancing. I love to dance; I like loud music, like to lose myself in a raucous beat until my mind recedes and I am just a collection of joints and limbs pulsing and swaying. People never expect it of me.

My friends had dragged me out to the club that night and I was feeling good out on the floor, dancing by myself. Dani came right up to me and just like that we fell into a rhythm with each other, as if our cells were perfectly in sync. I loved that feeling. When she told me where she worked I believed that she too was connected to the world, attuned to something bigger, something beyond the container of skin that is our humdrum life. But I was wrong about her. She quit her job and I went back to the news, like an old friend.

Now she wants a house and a baby and a life like Gina's and Natalie's and I subscribe to the daily editions of the Los Angeles Times and the New York Times. I subscribe to cable, so I can get CNN. I've programmed the buttons in my car to all the NPR stations. I am carried along on the current of events – wars and natural disasters, terrorist attacks and ecological breakdowns. These are what touch me.

O

Still not speaking, Dani pulls into our underground parking and we trudge up the concrete steps to our second floor unit. Dani is waiting for me to apologize, I know, and then she will chastise and forgive me, but I just can't. I will never be the way Dani wants me to be, oblivious to the civil war in the Sudan and the vanishing rain forests.

Once inside, I take off my dress and drape it indifferently over a hanger, not bothering to straighten its contours. I pull the clips out of my hair, let it fall across the tops of my shoulders. I brush my teeth and rinse my face with cold water.

Dani stands at the bathroom door, her eyes on me. The hard set of her mouth has softened; her gaze holds a question. My lack of apology, my refusal to back down has unnerved her, shifted the balance of power. She doesn't know what's going to happen next. So she comes up behind me, rests her cheek on my naked back. Her hands wrap around to cup my breasts, palms pressing my nipples. I feel simultaneously inside and outside of her embrace, even as I turn to face her, let her mouth find mine.

She is seeking reassurance as her tongue pushes toward mine, as she tosses her pressed slacks in a heap on the carpet and leads me to bed. I don't fault her for it. Even though my skin is thick as granite, my breath still quickens at the press of her teeth in the crook of my neck; I still grow wet at the weight of her hips against mine. It's my brain that is watching off to the side, an uninvolved bystander.

Making love with Dani is something I will miss; she is fiery and generous, playful, insistent. But as she holds me, as she wraps her legs around me and draws me closer, she cannot contain all that I am. She doesn't want to embrace the plane crash of my shoulders, the torture of detainees in my ribs, the diminishing polar ice caps of my thighs. Tonight, as her orgasm crests beneath my fingers, she dissolves in tears, her body already knowing what her mind has yet to admit. She has gone live on the other planet now, and I cannot follow her. I can't breathe in its atmosphere. I couldn't tell you the last time we went dancing. She falls asleep with her face resting against my heart.

I kiss her forehead as I gently disentangle myself and roll off the mattress, pausing at the bathroom door to slip into a robe – Dani's or mine, I can't tell in the dark. Barefoot, I pad into the dining room, take a seat at the table. My toes curl around the rungs of the wooden chair. The room glows with a grayish light from the street lamps beyond the window.

My eyes roam the space before me. I regard the apartment as if I've just come back, years after having moved away. The corner of the living room where Dani kept her treadmill. The shelves that used to house all my books. I am a visitor from the future, regarding my present life with nostalgia. I do not feel sad. Perhaps Arshille was right.

I try to remember the techniques I used to meditate, deepening my breath, closing my eyes. I try to find that whiteness in my brain, that silken pocket. At some point I must have put my head down in my arms because the next thing I know the sky is nearly light and I'm awakened by the sound of the Sunday Times thwacking its heft against the sidewalk.

Taking just a moment to plug in the coffeemaker, I climb downstairs to retrieve the paper. Back upstairs I hear the hiss and drip of coffee brewing. I hear Dani groan in sleep and imagine her reaching for me. Across the street, a neighbor backs down his drive, headlights on.

But all this dims and recedes, like a memory of childhood, or the address of a place one used to live, as my eyes catch the front page story about the execution of dissidents in China. The stone walls of my prison cell are always cold. I have had an ache in my chest ever since I arrived here, seven years ago, I think. Without turning on a lamp, in the eerie half-light of dawn, I begin to read the news.

temperance

"I don't drink."

It was an announcement, a declaration made, not in response to a particular question nor to any offer of refreshment, but out of the blue. She spoke the words with all the fervent resolve of a line scarred into the sawdust at our feet.

I had arrived only minutes before. It was one of the first things she told me about herself. Not the first thing, which was something about the neighborhood she lived in, nor the second, which was most likely about her job. Still, very little time had passed before she made it a point to let me know, "Oh, by the way, I don't drink."

"Excuse me?" Maybe the music had gotten louder, or maybe my attention had wandered.

"I don't drink," she repeated. She said it like a warning, or like a test. This was something she definitely wanted me to know if I was going to think about dating her.

It was a test I didn't think I was likely to pass, but I wasn't even sure I was interested in dating her. She was someone Eric knew, Eric from the office, and he kept saying to me he had this friend, I ought to give her a call. So one day I did, explaining about the office and about Eric, and I suggested we might meet at this little dive in my neighborhood.

She could have told me then, I guess, could have suggested some other place, and maybe she regretted that she hadn't. Maybe that's why she blurted it out like a secret she just couldn't keep.

She was cute enough, though not as tall as I usually like. Not really my physical type at all. She had that kind of thin blond hair that can look stringy if it's not washed often enough or not well shaped, but hers looked shiny and styled, cut blunt just below the line of her chin. I'd be lying if I said I knew the color of her eyes.

She seemed like a nice girl, and maybe that was the trouble. Nice girls always seem to get a little more unhappy when they hang around with me.

Her features were pleasant, maybe a little bland, but they grew noticeably sharper as she made her declaration. Her assertion hung in the air between us, like a smoke ring that refused to dissipate, until there seemed nothing for me to do but bite.

"Why not?" I asked like I wanted to know.

She didn't answer, but gave me a look. It was a look full of pre-dawn hangovers and DUI's, of trying to keep quiet while puking in the toilet at work. It was a look full of darkness and all the more bitter for it, and as I studied her gaze I knew suddenly, and with absolute certainty, that I could get her to drink, no problem. That very night, if I chose. It wasn't that I cared whether she drank or not, but I suddenly recognized that her announcement was not a test, but a dare, and I began to feel excitement for the first time since I'd arrived.

I leaned closer to her, extended a hand that grazed the fine hairs of her forearm. "That takes guts," I said to her, with the full-throated sincerity of an actor in his first big part.

She blinked twice; it was not the reaction she'd expected. I had caught her off-guard and it made her nervous. She shrugged one shoulder.

When the bartender approached, she ordered a club soda. Considerate, I asked, "Will it bother you..." before ordering a whiskey sour.

This is not what I ordinarily drink; I'm not sure I'd ever had a whiskey sour before that night, but I saw her give it an envious glance when it was set down before me and I knew my instincts were on-target.

She sucked hard on the straw plunged into her Collins glass of soda, and we commenced a desultory conversation, that kind of first-date chit-chat when neither party has decided if the other one's worth their while. She told me about her dog, Hector, a mutt she found on the street, how she had to bathe him everyday or else he smelled bad.

Who knows what I told her? Maybe some story about hitching to California when I was seventeen and never leaving. I was pretty sure I'd never told Eric I grew up here.

She must have decided that she liked me a little bit, because she started in on her last relationship, how it began, how it ended. We were on our second round, and I asked her casually, "Would you like the cherry?" I held out the blue plastic sword impaling the orange and the maraschino, glowing lurid red.

She hesitated, but I could tell she felt stupid, thought that to refuse would make her seem rigid and uptight, so she said, "I guess, thanks."

I'd made sure to give the sword an extra swirl in the top of my glass before handing it over, and her eyes widened as her tongue tasted the whiskey-soaked fruit.

"Thanks," she said again, and fidgeted with her cocktail napkin, tearing one long shred from its edge.

I took a sip from my glass, setting it down with an air of deep satisfaction. "They make a good whiskey sour," I declared, then said, "Oh, I'm sorry."

"It's okay," she assured me, if a little grimly.

Then I must have told her my own tale of lost love, something with plenty of tragedy; maybe it had an ocean as a backdrop. Her forehead creased in sympathy, and she lay a warm hand on top of mine.

At that point I excused myself, took a trip to the restroom. I wanted to leave her alone with my beverage, give her a chance to think. I took a long time, washing my hands under a stream of lukewarm water, passing a flat comb through my hair in front of the mirror.

When I returned, my glass was not on the same side of the napkin as I had placed it before getting up. I pretended to take no notice, re-seated myself on the bar stool, and asked, "Miss me?" with a winsome grin.

She returned a thin smile; I couldn't tell if it held guilt or sarcasm. Still, she seemed happy enough to see me, because the next topic of conversation was about her childhood. As these kinds of stories go, hers was neither the most harrowing nor the most joy-filled I'd been told. No overt brutality, no bucolic holidays. Just a mother who disappeared – mostly quietly – into a prescription drug addiction. She told it simply, with neither theatrical self-pity nor that tough fragility – a kind of calculated brittleness – I've seen some girls adopt. This made me almost like her; she seemed more vulnerable to me now, human, and I almost began to have second thoughts about my scheme to sway her resolve.

But by that time it had all gone beyond me. When the bartender returned to check on us, she piped up, "Make that two whiskey sours," as if the impulse had just occurred to her, as if she hadn't been thinking about it for the last half-hour or more, turning it over and over in her brain, a devil whispering into one ear, an angel in the other. I made sure my face conveyed just a hint of surprise, curiosity without judgment, and she offered a small shrug as if to say, "Nobody's perfect."

When the bartender set the drink before her she embraced it like an old friend, gripping the stem of the glass in a hearty grasp, and tossing back a full third of it in a single gulp. Her eyelids fluttered shut as she savored the taste of the booze and sweet lime; a tension eased out of her shoulders. She turned to me with a smile less tentative than before.

I might have expected to feel something then, a victory of confirmation at least, but the moment was anticlimactic. I understood then that it had been a foregone conclusion all along, having little to do with me, really. Whether it was an elaborate form of self-deception or a calculated strategy didn't really matter; this was a routine she had perfected through repetition. When I told the story to Eric the next day, he looked genuinely shocked, demanding, "How could you do that to someone? How can you live with yourself?" but I said, "Don't you see? I gave her someone to blame."

After her second drink she became quite flirtatious, scooting her bar stool close to mine, running her hand along my thigh, as if hidden mechanism of control had been sprung. Her voice grew louder, her stories more animated. She leaned her head on my shoulder and I felt her hot breath against my neck.

After we closed the bar I walked her home; it was the least I could do. She kept bumping her hip against mine as we walked the deserted blocks to her neighborhood; then she'd giggle and apologize. She'd become little-girlish, talking in a kind of feathery, whispery voice, as if I were someone bigger, older, someone with power over her, someone to beguile.

I could see the scene as it unfolded in her brain: how she'd relinquished her will to me, and now she was mine to do with what I liked. I saw how she'd woven me into her story, caught me up like a fish in a net. Soon I'd begin to stink. I was supposed to be the next stranger she woke up beside, the next item she'd add to her list of personal shortcomings.

But I was tired of her now.

When we reached her doorstep, she pushed her body against mine; her mouth reaching up for a kiss seemed like a bottomless cavern. Lightly, I pressed my lips to her forehead, a quick peck, not unfriendly but disengaged. Then I plucked the keys from her unsteady hand and released the lock to her bungalow apartment. I held the door for her and, once she'd entered, let it close gently behind her.

I was halfway down the courtyard when the door struggled open, and she leaned out into the mist-filled pre-dawn air. "Hey!" she called after me. Her voice was a mess of confusion. "Where're you going?"

"Home," I replied. "You get some sleep."

I didn't wait for her response, but turned and headed along the pavement, refusing to feel the eyes that followed my retreating back as it disappeared into the gray light of not-yet-morning.

a whisper in the veins

The apartment is small and ugly modern, and I stand tracking mud and melted snow onto the nondescript linoleum of its tiny kitchen. My mother rises from her rocking chair where she's been reading the paper, padding into the kitchen in her stockinged feet.

I stare at her feet as I remember a story she used to tell me when I was a child. "I always wanted to have fat feet," the story begins. "Mine were skinny and narrow and I thought it would be just wonderful to have fat feet." She never explained where this standard of beauty originated – she takes it for granted that anyone would understand the desire. "So one day I was walking outdoors and I stepped on a bee. I did it on purpose because I knew it would make my foot swell. What I didn't know is that it would be so painful!"

Her arms close around me and I lean down to kiss her cheek. She takes my coat and spreads a newspaper where I can leave my wet shoes. The darkened leather warns me that these Cole-Hahn loafers will never be the same. It wasn't snowing in D.C., where I started from this morning. I tell her I have only the afternoon, a more or less impulsive stopover on my way home from a business trip.

I follow her in my damp socks into the living room. I recognize a few of the pieces of furniture that I grew up with – an old desk, a large oak bureau, my father's stuffed green chair – but they seem unfamiliar in this square room. Against one wall a television is flickering, though the sound is turned down. It's not the same one that I last saw in my parents' house. Most of the furniture is new, bought from Sears or Montgomery Wards on time payments.

I sit in my father's chair. She is anxious and shy with me, bustling around making coffee, tidying up the scattered pieces of the newspaper, wanting to get me a sweater, though the room isn't cold. She asks if I need to go to the bathroom. I don't. I pick up the front page of the paper and retreat into reading it, sinking into news of a plane crash, a treaty negotiated, the predictions of a dire year for agriculture.

My mother brings me a cup of pale brown coffee. She's always made her coffee weak. "Looks like rain, but it smells like coffee," my father used to joke. She interrupts my reading to ask if I'd like some toast or a cinnamon roll. Monosyllabic, I indicate my preference for the former and begin studying Ann Landers' advice to a woman whose relatives criticize her housekeeping.

After I've scanned the comics, my mother pulls the card table over in front of my chair. The table is draped with a lacy crocheted table cloth, which covers a cotton cloth printed with red cherries. I remember the cherries from the kitchen table in my childhood. She sets a plate of toast on top and moves my coffee cup beside it. I lay the paper aside, pick up a heavily buttered slice of toast and dunk it in my coffee cup. This is something I do only when I'm with my mother. It is her custom, and in her house I observe it.

Little crumbs bob in the cup and a puddle of melted butter creates a rainbow slick on the surface of the coffee. The soaking bread dissolves easily in my mouth.

"How are you? Have you been healthy?," my mother asks, still shyly. This is an innocent question, standard in my mother's repertoire.

I nod, noncommittally. I'm caught off guard, and glance at her suspiciously. I've come here to tell her something, but I can't just blurt it out to her, not in this small ugly room with the television flickering.

My mother doesn't wait for an answer. Her attention has wandered to the screen, where characters in a soap opera act out their dramas. When I was a child I used to watch these with my mother when I'd stay home from school. I have friends who are too sick to work anymore and they stay home everyday and watch the soaps. When they're not talking about their symptoms or a new doctor or the latest experimental treatment, they talk about the stories on the soaps.

"Ericka's going to get what's coming to her now," my mother remarks, referring to the woman on the screen whose evil good looks invite fascination and loathing. I don't know what Ericka's got coming to her, but I can tell by looking at her she has karmic debts to pay. I've heard Jerry and Stuart talk about Ericka, but since I don't follow the soaps I've never paid much attention.

"How've you been feeling, Mom?," I change the subject.

She starts a little, shifts her attention back to me, and blinks behind her glasses. My mother's never worn glasses before, I realize, and she's picked out a really stupid pair, ones which are not flattering to her face or coloring. They're also at least ten years out of fashion.

It makes me crazy when my mother's cheap. I know that my father left her a comfortable sum of money, but here she is in a drab apartment, shopping at Sears and buying tacky polyester pantsuits and stupid glasses. I really ought to take her shopping.

I used to do that when I was younger. My father was appalled, but as a fifteen-year-old boy I liked nothing better than to take my mother shopping. We'd drive over to one of the better department stores – I always insisted on that – and spend the afternoon amid the racks of women's sportswear, Better Dresses, Town and Country. My mother was amazed that I had such a sense of women's clothing; I knew fabrics, lines, designer labels. She always swore I had better taste than she did. My mother was still an attractive woman then, and I loved to make her look gorgeous.

Now she has terrible glasses and a bad perm. This makes me sad. It's been a couple of years since I've seen her – the last time was at my father's funeral.

"Oh, I'm all right, I guess. I have such a hard time sleeping," she complains softly in answer to my question. "And I still have these stomach pains when I eat."

"Didn't the doctor tell you to stop drinking coffee?" She has told me this about her stomach in several of our phone conversations. I've tried to call her more regularly since my father died.

"Well, yes, but I don't drink it very much." She is distracted; she really wants to find out what's going to happen to Ericka.

My mother and I were very close until I was about nineteen. That's when I told her I was gay. She took it hard, a lot harder than my father. I suppose he had always known. It disgusted him, but it wasn't a surprise. I think my mother blamed herself. Maybe she heard my father's hundreds of admonishments – "You're spoiling him, Mae" – and took them to heart for the first time.

Anyway, we'd said some terrible things to each other then, and I upped and moved to L.A. My parents became a distant memory, a photograph. I'd send presents at Christmas and cards on birthdays, but they had no part in my daily life.

The soap ends and my mother moves across the room and presses the button that turns the TV off. The picture disappears from the screen, collapsing in on itself, and the room is suddenly darker. She shuffles to the other corner of the room and turns on a lamp. I recognize the lamp from my father's den in the old house, but as with the other familiar objects in the room, it is unfamiliar here.

"Do you want some more coffee?," she asks awkwardly, standing by the window with its cheap lace curtains, "or some more toast? Can I make you a tuna sandwich?" She's happy to see me, but doesn't know exactly what to do with me.

"Let's play some cards," I suggest, and she smiles in relief. She indicates for me to lift my plate and saucer, then she peels the crocheted cloth off the table, revealing more fully the faded splendor of the printed cherries below. She goes to the bureau and slides open a drawer, easily finding the deck in its proper place. She pulls a folding chair to the opposite side of the card table and sits.

The cards are well-worn – I recognize the deck with its illustration of hunting dogs on the back. The game is gin rummy, the continuation of a ritual begun in my early childhood. Whenever I'd be home sick, or on nights when my father didn't get home on time, or on holidays when there was no place to go, even on the night of my father's funeral after the guests had gone home – my mother and I would compete for the Gin Rummy Championship of the World.

She liked to devise an elaborate score sheet, with three games at once. If you won a hand, your score was entered in the first game. When you won another hand, that was added to your earlier total while at the same time got you entered into the second game.

Gin rummy brings out a competitive streak that is seldom seen otherwise in either of our personalities. My mother is a cutthroat card player, and she'll watch with cunning which cards I pick up, which I discard, and plan her strategy accordingly.

I spread my hand open in front of my face and sort through: a pair of a dark Kings and the Jack of Spades – I can play that either way, hoping for a third King or the Queen of Spades. I have the four, five, six of clubs. Nothing else to speak of, but I can build from there.

"You," I announce, waving my cards at her, "have dealt me a

supreme hand!" We bluff to torment one another. "You really ought to shuffle better."

"One card," she teases back. "Just give me one card."

I once taught this game to Stuart, during one of the bad periods when he was bedridden. It had been hard for him to concentrate and he was easy to beat. I'd felt guilty about winning, but didn't know how not to.

My mother's brow is furrowed as she tries to decide whether to pick up the Jack of Spades I just discarded or take her chances from the deck. She chooses a new card and her face lights up.

"I'm going to knock with four points!" she crows triumphantly, spreading her cards on top of the cherries.

I lay down my three Kings, my four, five, six of clubs. I have two deuces which I toss to the side to offset her four points. I'm still holding the eight of hearts and the ace of Diamonds.

"Nine points," I say glumly. She gleefully records this on her score sheet.

As she deals again I watch her hands. I've always loved my mother's hands. They are strong still and heavily veined, spotted now with age but agile as she flips the cards into a pile in front of me.

As has been our custom now for many years, she asks me nothing about my life. "How's your job?" she'll say, expecting and gratified to hear, "Oh, about the same." She'll ask about my house – I've sent her pictures of the Spanish-style home in the Hollywood Hills where Robert and I used to live together – but not about what it's like to live there alone now, or if in fact I am living there alone.

I win the next hand – all the right cards just come to me, as they always seem to do when I don't care about winning – with an extra 25 points for ginning. I don't know how I'm going to say what I've come all this way to tell her. She already asked about my health, but I was caught off-guard.

She wants to know if I've seen any movies and we talk about the latest releases. Some of my favorites are independents that won't make it to this part of the country. Outside the window I can see it starting to snow more heavily; the afternoon is growing dark.

She tells me that my cousin Lenore, her sister's daughter, has had a baby, a boy. She named it Gregory, which is my name, but also my grandfather's. I tell her something cute that my dog Jackson did recently. She smiles vaguely, she doesn't know a lot about dogs.

When Robert got sick, he had to call his parents in Waco, Texas and tell them for the first time that he was gay. I remember lying in bed that morning, watching his neck flush and the muscles of his back tense as he listened to first his mother, then his father tell him that his illness was God's punishment. That they would pray for him. They never came to visit during those weeks when Robert was in the hospital, and I couldn't decide who he needed me to be most – his lover or his parent.

I want to tell my mother this story, as she quickly grasps the Queen of Diamonds and positions it in her hand. She discards the five of spades and I pick it up, although I have no use for it at all.

I'm playing recklessly now, totally without strategy, picking up and discarding with no thought for the consequences. When my mother wins, I'm holding seventy-three points in my hand.

She looks at me over the top of those unflattering frames and complains, "You're not concentrating! It's not fun if you make it so easy for me!" She dutifully records that she's won the first game and is perilously close to taking the second as well.

I deal, shuffling the cards automatically. I'm thinking about my test, just a couple of weeks ago, about the earnest counselor who gave me my results. She was wearing green eye shadow that was a bad color for her skin tone, and made more prominent the deep circles under her eyes.

My mother takes this hand easily and throws down her cards in disgust. "You're worse than your father!," she snorts.

My father was a terrible cards player. He was a cabinet maker, as his father had been, as so many men had once been in this lumber-rich part of the country. He trusted the grain of wood, the burls and knots, what he could see and shape with his own hands. The abstract patterns of clubs and diamonds and their possibilities were never real to him.

"I'm sorry." I smile, conciliatory. I glance at my watch. "I've got a couple more hours. Can I take you out for an early dinner somewhere nice?"

She looks out the window, where the blizzard is raging. "Do you think your plane will really take off?" She sounds both hopeful and fearful. "It's a real Michigan night." Her tone turns apologetic, as if she is afraid she's disappointing me. "I don't really feel like going out in all that. Why don't I just heat up a couple of Lean Cuisines in the microwave?"

I nod my assent, uncomfortably aware of the time passing. She gets up, gathers the cards into their pack before she asks, "You're done with these, aren't you?" I nod again. She returns them to their place in the bureau drawer on her way to the kitchen. I hear her opening the freezer.

"Where's the phone?," I want to know.

"It's in the bedroom. You'll see it. Don't you want to call Derek?" Derek was a friend of mine in high school, someone I haven't seen since I moved away. My mother's run into him with his family a couple of times at the mall. "Or Elsa? She'll never forgive me if she hears you were in town and didn't call her." Elsa is my aunt, her sister.

"I'm just going to call the airlines and see if my plane is still taking off tonight." I wish I could keep the testiness out of my voice.

I step into her bedroom and am struck by the familiar scent of White Shoulders, the perfume my mother has always worn. Most of the furniture is the same as it was in the house I grew up in – the bed frame, the dresser, the dressing table. Missing is the large armoire that my father built, that housed his things.

I sit on the new rose-colored comforter. It's stuffed with fiberfill, not down – my mother's cheapness again. The phone by the bed is a new thing; my father would never have put up with that. He had an inherent distrust of telephones, to him they were a vehicle for public, not private, communication. On the rare times he called me in California, probably not more than three times in the fifteen years I've lived there, he always delivered his message quickly, in a self-conscious truncated voice. And he always refused to leave a message if he got an answering machine.

An airline attendant with a flat Michigan accent informs me that the planes are flying, and on schedule. Looking outside at the blizzard I find this hard to believe, but I will it to be true. I glance at my watch – I should phone for a cab in about an hour.

I raise the window blind and press my nose to the cold glass. A circle of steam clouds the place where my nose has been. I trace a pattern into it, then watch it disappear as the steam evaporates.

Before leaving the bedroom, I stop to stare at a framed photo on the dressing table. It's a picture of my mother and father when they were in their early thirties, before I was born. She is sitting on his lap, her arms clasped around his neck. His head is thrown back. They are both laughing with abandon, in adoration, perhaps with lust. I never knew my parents like this but I love the photograph. I love knowing that for at least one moment in their lives they felt like this with each other.

Reluctantly I go back to the living room. On the card table my mother has set out plates of bread; plastic containers of bean salad, cole slaw, cottage cheese; dishes of canned fruit in heavy syrup. The table is set and I stand there, not knowing what to do.

"Is your plane leaving?," she calls from the kitchen.

"Hard to believe, but they swear it's even on time. I should call a cab after we eat."

She sticks her head out of the kitchen. I'm struck by the mixture of regret and relief in her voice as she says, "It's too bad you're here such a short time. Are you sure you can't spend the night?"

I explain again about the clients I have to meet in L.A. in the morning. She bobs her head; she doesn't understand the laws of commerce, but she knows better than to think she can interrupt them.

"Go and wash you hands now. We're ready to eat." She shoos me toward the bathroom as the microwave begins to beep.

The liquid soap won't lather in my hands, as I rub them together under a trickle of warm water. I stare at my face in the bathroom mirror. The blonde profile, the tanned skin, the good haircut, all serve to hide the shadow that whispers in my veins.

Tell her, I command the face in the mirror. Do what you've come to do. I nod in agreement, then turn to wipe my hands on the ridiculous tiny pink guest towels my mother has carefully displayed on the rack.

Ever the hostess, my mother has spooned everything from the Lean Cuisine trays onto plates, arranged it like a meal she has really cooked. The television is on again, this time with the sound.

"I hope you don't mind," she apologizes, indicating the screen. "I like to watch the news."

A man in a checkered suit so bad it's comic is drawing in chalk on a map – the local station here can't afford the fancy computer graphics that are routinely used to foretell the weather in L.A. He's chattering on about high pressure systems, storms from the north, wind chill factors.

I chew the bland food, better than airline food I have to admit, but only by degrees. My mother laughs at some joke made by the weather man.

When the sports report comes on I think I have a chance to get her attention. "Mom?" I venture.

She turns to me, already anticipating what she thinks I'm going to say. She's out of her seat, saying, "You want more milk? Can I get you anything else? Are you ready for some coffee? I have a nice pumpkin pie and a Dutch apple from the store – I can heat them up for us?"

"Mom, please just sit down!" My voice is harsher than I mean it to be. "I have something to say to you."

An edge creeps over her face, but she sits as I've asked her to. The national news report has just begun, and I can feel her urgent need to turn her attention there.

I once had to tell my mother about having broken the pocket watch that had belonged to her grandfather. I was about eight. It was real gold. She hadn't given me the watch yet; she told me she was keeping it for me until I was older and could appreciate its value. I kept taking it out to look at it and play with it until finally, somehow, I broke the crystal. I was sure it was irreparable and I was torn with guilt over destroying something that was precious to my mother. I didn't sleep the whole night before and when I finally told her, I cried. She was extremely kind. She said the watch could be fixed and that as soon as it was she would give it to me, since I had obviously learned to appreciate its worth.

When I was nineteen I told her I was gay. I was madly in love with Michael, a boy I'd met at college, and I expected her to share my elation. She instead responded that she was sickened, she hadn't raised me to be "that way," she was ashamed to call me her son.

After Robert died last year I called to tell her. "I don't know what to say," she'd said. "I don't understand, but I'm sorry if you hurt."

She sits before me now, her brown eyes cloudy behind her glasses. Her cheeks are soft and lined and tinged with rouge; her permed hair frizzes softly over her forehead. She still goes every two weeks to the beauty parlor, has it tinted a light brown.

She is my mother. She is seventy-one. Her husband is dead and she has one child, who lives in California. I think of all the ways we are known to each other, all the ways in which we are unknown.

Bravely, she speaks first. "What is it, Greg? What is it you want to tell me?" I see in her face a determination to hear whatever it is, and I love her fiercely for this.

I open my mouth, but the words that follow take me by surprise. "I want you to come to California. I want you to come and stay with me. I'll send you a ticket."

This is not what she expected either, whatever that might have been. She relaxes a little while she demurs. She's afraid to fly, especially with all the things that have been happening lately, the plane crashes, the hijackings. She sees them on the news. And she can't get away. She has her doctors' appointments. She helps Lenore out by watching the baby a few times a week. And what would she do in California anyway? She'd just be in the way.

"No," I contradict her, growing more insistent. "You should come right away. Get out of this winter! Come see my house! We'll go shopping! I'll send you a ticket this week!" I am seized with urgency.

She's overwhelmed. It's been years since I demanded anything of her. For this reason, more than any other, she agrees.

"I guess I could take a couple of weeks. But not next week – I get my hair done next week. I'll come the week after that." Her head is already full of plans: cancel the newspaper; get Mrs. Fletcher across the hall to bring in the mail; use up the food in the refrigerator so it doesn't go bad..

I sit back in my father's chair, full of surprise and accomplishment, though this is not what I had intended to accomplish. My news seems less important, somehow, than this plan.

I see it is time for me to start out for the airport. I go into the next room and call for a cab. Peering out the window I see that the snow has stopped, and the night beyond is cold and blue. Perhaps they'll have the runways cleared after all.

As I wait for the cab I help her wash the supper dishes. She washes, I dry and put away, just like when I was a kid. In what seems a very short time I hear the beep of a horn and see from the window a pair of headlights in the driveway below.

My coat is toasty from the heating vent where it's been drying all afternoon. My shoes are mottled, stiff and uncomfortable as I slip them on.

"Remember," I say as I give her a quick embrace, "I'm taking you shopping at Neiman Marcus." She giggles like a girl and I shut the door behind me.

sex less

Your herbalist swears it's *Qi* deficiency.

Your best friend accuses you of going back to men.

Your therapist tells you you're acting out, rebelling against mom.

Your gynecologist insists you're depressed.

Your lover's convinced that it's all her fault.

Everyone has an opinion, so eager to give you advice, though you never asked for it. Each is sure she can solve your problem, even if you don't think you have one.

They don't get it.

But why should they? Here, in the closing moments of the twentieth century – after five thousand years of patriarchal rule, five thousand years of being owned and sold and traded and bred like cattle, five thousand years of being defined as wanton and evil or as sexless, devoid of desire – women have stolen back sexuality. It's happened in your very lifetime: from the Pill to the Sexual Revolution, from vibrators to sex clubs, from *Our Bodies, Our Selves* to *on our backs,* women have spent the last thirty years reclaiming lust as a birthright. How could any sane lesbian renounce it?

You say: you're tired. You've done more than your share of sucking and fucking, moaning and throbbing, creaming and cumming for one lifetime. Now you're content to think of it as something that you used to do, like drugs or the Hustle. Now it seems more like your favorite Motown song from the sixties after it's been played to death on the Classic Soul Oldies station: it no longer makes you wanna dance.

You're strangely not upset about this. It's everyone else who's upset.

Your best friend asks, "Is it Angela? Maybe you and Angela should go to couples' counseling."

Your gynecologist says, "Ten years is a long time to be with the same woman. Maybe you need to be non-monogamous for a while."

Your herbalist brews you a potion so strong that, once you drink it, you smell it in your sweat for days.

Your therapist suggests you up your appointments to three times a week.

Their efforts bemuse you. Nobody ever tried to intervene during those years you brought home from the bar a different woman each week. No one even blinked when you had three lovers at the same time and cried on the phone every day at work. None of them seemed concerned about too much sex.

And yet, when you think back on those years of chemistry and cruising, all that groping and straining and saliva, you can't help wondering – what was the point? Night after night of dissolving into neural explosion – does that constitute a life? Now it seems the body was not home but a mask, and you long to step out from behind it.

Angela is beside herself. She cannot see that this has nothing to do with your love for her, nothing to do with wanting anyone else. Her dark eyes follow you, ponds swollen with spring rain. She questions you whenever you return home: did you meet someone? Fear changes the shape of her beautiful mouth.

You wish you could explain it, to her, to the worried others, even to yourself. You search for words that would form themselves into the precise shape of your history, a bulk and density that pulls like gravity at your flesh, but the flesh is mute as lead, and the words fall to the ground in heaps, unformed, unheard.

She cannot, as you can, imagine a love relieved of the weight of lovemaking, a love as light and full as breath. You trace the curve of her hipbone and know that she will leave. You already miss the smell of her hair.

○

Your therapist recommends that you lie on the couch, abandon the upright safety of the chair; she wants you to go back, to walk again the long road of bodies that has led you to this spot. It embarrasses you to remove your shoes, you who's gone topless at the public beach, nude at music festivals, who has rarely overlooked an opportunity for sex in a bar restroom or a parked car on a busy street. Your stockinged feet feel naked here in the small air conditioned room.

Oblivious to chronology, you begin with a story from about ten years ago, just before you met Angela. You were at a party, given by someone who worked with you at the sound studio. The party was full of musicians and engineers and hangers-on, not so different from being at work. When the blonde with one walled eye walked in she noticed you immediately. You recognized her; you'd been with her before, uncountable years earlier. You hadn't liked her, you remembered, not before and not then, her personality as sharp and pointy as her face. Still, before the party was over, you'd had sex with her in the shower of the California bungalow's sole bathroom.

Your therapist asks, inevitably, "And how did you feel after you were with her?"

You are bored by the story, not just this chapter but the whole saga. You seem to yourself a cartoon figure, a female Bullwinkle with a permanent hard-on that you followed like a compass arrow. You remember more of the faces than you would have predicted, more of the names. You can recall certain details, the black tile that lined the shower, the blonde's scream of laughter as it shrilled in your ear, but you can't seem to recall the sensations that coursed through your body, lighting up neurons like a pinball machine, the explosions and whistles.

"Maybe we're all programmed to endure only so many orgasms," you suggest, "and I've used up my quota." It's as if you're recounting a story that was told to you, nothing you ever witnessed, your voice low and uninflected. Your eyes study a crack in the ceiling, try to follow it to its source.

○

Your best friend invites you to dinner, lures you with her offer to make spaghetti with clam sauce, her grandmother's recipe. Her girlfriend's away on business, Angela has been working late for the past month. "Just the two of us," your best friend urges.

You arrive with a bottle of wine, expecting to see the dining room table set for two. Instead, places have been laid on the coffee table, in front of the big screen TV. "I've got a surprise for you," your friend announces before disappearing back to the kitchen.

As the spaghetti steams on a plate before you, the tender clams redolent of cream and garlic, the wine pale in a thin-stemmed glass, your best friend pops a black cassette into the VCR. An image rises before you, a naked brunette climbs atop a naked redhead, pink flesh dragging across pink flesh, the focus is soft, the lighting is dim, and close-ups of breasts and stomachs and thighs and buttocks threaten to come rolling out of the screen into the living room.

"What is this?" you ask your friend. The soundtrack gasps and moans like a tired accordion. The brunette is plunging her fist into the redhead's vagina, inserting her arm past the wrist, her elbow pumping.

It's pornography," she tells you. She explains that she and her girlfriend often watch it to "put themselves in the mood."

"It's gonna make me spit up my dinner," you warn. Glumly, she turns clicks the remote, and the images collapse into blessed darkness.

"This is serious," she suddenly explodes. "It's not like you're eighty years old. You're way too young to lose your sex drive."

○

Apparently your gynecologist agrees, because she calls you at home. This strikes you as odd, but then she says, "I've been thinking a lot about this thing you've got going on with your libido. I want you to come into my office for a consultation."

You try to protest until, misunderstanding your reluctance, she proclaims, "I won't even charge you for an office visit. I've run across some information I think you'll find interesting."

You show up the next Tuesday morning, an eight a.m. appointment since you still hope to be on time for work. Your gynecologist greets you in her office, not an examination room, and pulls out a file folder marked "Testosterone."

Inside are photocopies of half a dozen articles, their type gray and fuzzy, regarding the use of this hormone to stimulate the libido of menopausal and post-menopausal women. You notice the articles all seem to be from popular women's magazines, not scientific journals. They are full of glowing testimonials from women who found that "sex is better than ever" and "now I want it almost every day" since the treatment.

You've been seeing your gynecologist for years. You originally chose her specifically because she is a lesbian. She has told you that she jettisoned her long-term relationship once the sex waned. She's now involved with a woman twenty-three years her junior.

You stare at your gynecologist across the desk. "Testosterone?" you ask. The bile in your tone wipes the self-congratulatory grin from her face.

O

Does it seem to you that everyone's gone crazy?

You're trying to explain this to your herbalist, when she takes your hand in her moist palms. She moves her chair closer, stares deep into your eyes.

"What my guides are telling me," she begins in the disembodied voice which means she's going metaphysical on you, "is that this whole situation with your sexuality represents a creative block that you're wrestling with."

You hate it when she brings her "guides" into it. She's a terrific herbalist; she's gotten rid of your PMS and your hay fever, and moved you through a couple of bouts of flu, but you'd just as soon stay on the physical plane, in the realm of the observable.

You never meant to work on this with her. It just came up one day during an examination; she was studying your tongue, its color, shape and coat, when she asked, "What's your level of sexual activity these days?" So you told her.

Now you're sorry. You've been privy to the havoc of her own romantic life, and are certain she's not the one you would turn to for this sort of advice.

"For years you've been facilitating the music of others," she intones as if dictating the words being channeled through her, "Now it's time for your to allow your own music to spill forth."

"You need to learn to trust yourself, your creativity." Her eyes flutter behind her thick glasses. Your herbalist is a frustrated painter, too busy always, she insists, to do what she swears she longs to do. If her "guides" are speaking, you believe, then this must be a message for her.

O

It is only Angela you can't dismiss. One night you arrive home and she's dressed in red bustier and garter belt, long black stockings. She's taken extra care with her make-up, piled her dark hair on top of her head.

Her breasts threaten to spill from their padded cups; a saxophone throbs from the stereo speakers.

She looks so like a little girl in borrowed clothes, imitating something she saw in her mother's movie star magazines, that you want to laugh. But you know this effort is all for you and instead you begin to cry.

At first she's confused at the sight of your tears; she straddles your lap, attempts to cajole you. You remember how your body once opened to hers. You tell yourself to reach for her. You've slept with many women in your life without feeling it, what could it hurt? But you know that Angela will not be fooled by a cheap show of technique; Angela will search your eyes and find you missing. And besides, you just can't make your body lie anymore.

You cry harder, watch the realization spread across her face that she's once more failed to win you. Her eyes narrow, the jaw hardens, her humiliation masked with fury. Her high heels click out of the room, recede down the hall. You hear water running in the bathroom, the sound of clothes slammed back into drawers. The saxophone evaporates into air.

○

Your mother once told you that she never had sex again after she turned forty.

"Didn't you miss it?" you'd asked at the time. You were twenty-seven then and the revelation shocked you. You thought sex was like vitamins, a daily dose essential to your health.

"I was relieved," she confided. "I never liked it all that much. I think your father found— other ways to get it. He needed it more. I just told him not to tell me, and it was fine." There was not a shade of regret in her voice.

You wondered then if it wasn't a matter of generation, your mom born in a time when women weren't expected to like it, when the predominant values were duty and sacrifice, not gratification and individual fulfillment. Back then, you strutted your era's freedoms like a badge of superiority.

Your mother is now almost seventy. Your dad has been dead for twelve years. You stare into her still-blue eyes and find serenity. She has her garden, her book group; your brother has given her grandchildren.

Her life is full; she is content. There is no chance of finding porn tapes on her coffee table or testosterone in her medicine cabinet.

○

Another friend calls you; she's been celibate for six months. She groans into the phone receiver, complains that she's "horny." Your try to imagine your mother horny; it's impossible.

You wonder if it isn't something to do with lesbians, with definition. If a woman is queer because she has sex with her own gender, then pride and propaganda requires she have sex as often as possible, an affirmation of identity. Maybe that's what you've been doing all those years. And without sex, who do you become?

Maybe that's what riles your best friend, what worries your gynecologist. They see you as a defector, not holding up your end of the queer covenant.

Any of them might be right – therapist, herbalist, gynecologist, friend. Perhaps you should be as distressed as they, scrambling to shore up your sexual identity. You wonder whether this change is permanent, if, like your mother, you should take up gardening. Odd, that even this prospect doesn't frighten you.

Stretched out in the bath, you stare at your naked body, the skin surprisingly unmarked from its years on the battle lines. You examine the parts–breasts and pubis and thighs – once the sites of desire, but now they seem without landmark, the old maps obsolete.

Beyond the door, Angela moves about the house, making her preparations for sleep. Rejection rings in her every step; you hear bitterness in the way she pulls back the sheet. You'd like to call to her, tell her how much you cherish her laughter, and the way she cries at movies and during sappy commercials, the heat of her skin in sleep, but she won't hear you now.

Submersed in the steaming water, you cup your small breast. Your nipple does not harden, nerves do not ignite. You feel only a vague comfort, like an arm wrapped around you in sleep. You sigh, settle back against porcelain, steeped in the relief of feeling nothing.

48 years after the crash

Gina had little use for her cousin's side of the family; the whole lot of them seemed insufferably wholesome and normal. There were no divorces, no alcoholism, no brawls, no child abuse on that branch of the family tree. Or at least none that she knew of. So she'd always assumed they had nothing in common with her.

Her cousin Garrett was a lawyer. He lived Charlotte, North Carolina, and for a living he defended corporations against labor disputes, affirmative action and civil rights cases. Despite her contempt for his side of the family, despite being appalled by how he earned his money, Gina could not help liking Garrett. He always reminded her of James Taylor, benign and good-hearted and sexy in a folksy, understated way.

She'd last seen Garrett, in Charlotte, seven years ago when she'd visited her grandfather – their grandfather – in a nursing home. The family wasn't from the South, none of them were, but her aunt and uncle had relocated there due to one of her uncle's big promotions. They'd ended up caring for her grandfather after her grandmother died.

That time, in Charlotte, she'd gone to dinner with her aunt, and Garrett, and Garrett's girlfriend at the time, whose name and personality Gina could no longer remember. They'd eaten at one of those pseudo-Mexican restaurants, the kind you find in parts of the country where there are few Mexicans, where the salsa is made from a ketchup base, and Garrett kept teasing her about not drinking. "How do you relax?," he'd asked incredulously.

"I'm a New Yorker. I don't." She had to admit she'd been curt. Since childhood it had been her position to remain aloof from any overtures from this branch of her family. If they wanted to go ahead and be cheerleaders and play golf and live in the suburbs, that was their business. It had nothing to do with her.

Garrett wrote occasional letters, which always surprised her. She couldn't imagine why he would seek her out. Unless all that normalcy really didn't pay off for him, and he wanted a glimpse of what was on the other side. But Gina was no tour guide. She didn't have time to fill in the chinks or provide the kinks in someone's humdrum existence. She never answered the letters.

And now they were in Illinois for her grandfather's – their grandfather's – funeral. Illinois because that's where he'd been born – though he hadn't been back in fifty years – and because that's where Gina's mother had arranged to have him buried. Gina had not planned to come to the funeral. She'd said good-bye to him on that visit seven years ago.

Her grandfather had been manic-depressive since his thirties. Most of the time when she was growing up he'd been stuck in a manic phase – cheerful, talkative, energetic – but a massive stroke had pulled the plug on that. For the last several years he hadn't spoken to or even seemed to recognize anyone.

"There's no point in my coming to the funeral," Gina told her mother when she received the call. "The truth is, he's been gone for a long time."

"That's just terrible. You're so heartless." Gina could tell from her mother's voice that she'd been drinking. Well, it was 3 p.m. Gina normally had a policy of never speaking to her mother past noon.

"I'm not heartless. It's a relief that he's dead. He hasn't even talked to anybody since 1980. When I went to see him at the home he never even got out of his chair. He just stared at the TV screen the whole time. Soap operas, game shows, cartoons, commercials – it was all the same to him."

Her mother started to cry. "It's all my fault. I never should have let Ellen talk me into putting him in that home. And all the way down in North Carolina!" Ellen was her mother's sister, Gina's aunt, Garrett's mother.

Gina held the receiver a little way away from her ear. Her mother could really work up a good wail when she'd had a few drinks.

After she calmed down, her mother pleaded, "So you'll come? For me?"

"No, I have an important client on Friday. Look, all of Ellen's family will be there. No one will even miss me. I'll send some flowers, okay?"

Gina had thought this would be the end of it. She'd immediately phoned Patrick, her neighborhood florist, and wired a large arrangement, sparing no expense. Then she put it out of her mind.

She'd been caught off guard by the call from Garrett. She couldn't remember if they'd ever talked on the phone in their lives.

"Gina, this is your cousin Garrett," is how he began the conversation. She felt a twinge of malicious glee as she heard the way the South had crept into his voice.

"Garrett, how the hell are you?" She made herself sound bored.

"You've heard about Grandpa, haven't you?" He knew damn well that she had. She'd lay money that he'd just gotten off the phone with her mother.

"Yeah. I can't say I'm too shook up about it though. He's been sort of a vegetable for years."

"Gina!" He sounded shocked and hurt but he recovered. "I'm calling to ask you to come to the funeral."

What's it to you, she wanted to ask, but said instead, "I already told Mom; I'm not doing it. My grandfather checked out of his hotel a long time ago. Just because his heart finally caught up to the rest of him is no reason for me to drop everything to fly to Illinois for a gathering of the tribe." She paused to let this sink in. "Besides, I have to meet with a big client. I'm shooting the cover for a new magazine called *Bang.*"

"Gina." He sounded so patient and empathetic she wanted to strangle him. It was the sort of tone one used with children, or with mental patients who are acting up. "I know you have your own reasons for not wanting to be with the family, but I'm asking you to come for me. I haven't seen you in seven years. And before that it was God knows how long. I feel like you're part of my family and I don't even know you."

"Garrett, some things it's better not to know. Count your blessings!"

"Damn, you're a hard one! Gina, I'd like to see you. This is an opportunity. Please come. If money's a problem, I'd be happy to pay for your ticket."

Although money was not a problem at this particular minute – she'd been shooting a lot of commercial jobs lately, she was sort of a hot photographer at the moment – she figured, hell, he's got more of it than he knows what to do with. She smiled as she retorted, "Well, if you feel that way about it, let's meet in Rio."

She could feel his grin at the other end of the line; his lawyer's instinct told him he was going to win. "Shall I make you a reservation?"

"Sure, go ahead. Never let it be said that I couldn't be bought! I'll fly in Friday morning, I don't care how early, just don't book me out of Newark. And I'll come back on the last flight Friday night."

"Gee, are you sure you can spare all that time?"

"Listen, don't push your luck. It's a stretch as it is. Oh, and I have to sit on the aisle. And I have to rent a car, but I'll pay for that."

"Why don't you just let me pick you up? I'm going in Thursday with Mom and Dad. I'll get you Friday morning and take you back Friday night."

"No way. I want to be sure I can make a quick getaway."

"Well, I just want to make sure we have some time to see each other."

"Right. That's what you're paying for. Don't worry, I'll see you get your money's worth."

"Gina, you're just terrible."

"Yes. I am."

○

She now sat across from Garrett in the dim blue light of a bar, somewhere on the road to the airport. Outside it was blowing snow, and the airline was reporting a two-hour delay in the departure time. It had been Garrett's idea to call the airport in advance. Gina would have been just as happy to be sitting on one of those hard molded plastic chairs underneath the fluorescent lights, reading People magazine.

She was dressed, as she had been all day, in a black leather two-piece suit with a mini-skirt. Her mother had been scandalized, but Gina had considered it the closest thing to appropriate funeral garb she owned. She often wore it to client meetings.

She was nursing a club soda – Perrier was too exotic for this joint. Garrett was on his second vodka and tonic, and he had just finished polishing off an enormous hamburger. Gina wasn't in the mood to eat anything.

He looked very much the way she remembered him – tall and athletic, handsome in an imperfect way, dressed impeccably in a tailored navy blue suit. She never met men like this. Gina met artists who painted naked women spread-eagled and sold their work in the high five-figures. She met club bouncers who wore chains. She met dope dealers, or out-of-work musicians waiting to cut a record that would blast them to the top of the charts. She met men who were gay. Or mean. Or both.

She sat back on the cracked vinyl seat and pulled a hand through her short bleached hair. Her roots were growing in, creating a dark corona at the base of her scalp from which the platinum spikes stretched in every direction. She sighed and checked her watch.

The day had been unremarkable, yet both remarked on it. They had discussed the flowers – Patrick had done his job beautifully; hers had been the classiest arrangement there. They spoke of the service (Him: "Really quite touching." Her: "A big bore. What a blowhard that reverend was."), how each family member had seemed. With considerable effort, Gina refrained from making snide comments about his sisters. There was still another two hours before the plane was scheduled to leave. If it ended up grounded for the night, Gina vowed to kill herself.

For a while they talked about Garrett's life – how he hated his job but really didn't know what else he wanted to do. He wanted to play sports; that's about all he really enjoyed, but he was too old now for a professional career. He felt stuck. He sounded genuinely miserable, as if there were some key that he had lost and was therefore locked out of contentment. It was hard for Gina to work up much sympathy.

She asked him about the girlfriend she'd met before, in North Carolina. She still couldn't remember the woman's name. It didn't matter; they'd been broken up for years. He was dating someone now who was all right, but not really special.

"So Garrett, cut the crap. What's this all about? Why did you pay for me to fly here to sit in this dive with you? Why do you write me those letters? It would be just as easy to pretend I don't exist. I just don't get it." Gina looked directly at him as she said this. Then she abruptly stopped and fiddled with the short red plastic straw sticking out of her club soda.

"Gina, I don't understand you. You're so hostile. I've never met a woman who's as angry as you. I don't even know what I did to you. I feel like you want to punish me for something." Garrett's brown eyes shone as if they had tears in them.

"Garrett, you don't know a damn thing." Her voice was weary and hopeless. She stuck two fingers into her glass and began fishing for ice cubes. These she popped into her mouth and demolished in loud crunches.

He reached over and took her hand. It was wet and cold. "I know that," he said. "You think I don't know that?"

She stared at her hand in his, thinking how ludicrous the whole thing was. His hand was warm and smooth. Out of habit, she imagined looking through the lens of a camera at this tableau. His nails were manicured. Hers were bitten stubs with red welts around the cuticles where she'd torn away hangnails. It made her laugh, though a little bitterly.

"Something's funny?" Garrett asked, stiffening as if instinctively protecting himself.

She shook her head and took her hand back. "Only to my twisted sense of humor." She was quiet for a moment, her eyes on the blue neon over the bar. Then she said, "Garrett, you don't know anything about me."

"Well, that's just what I was trying to say…" he interrupted but she stopped him.

She leaned her head back against the fake leather of the booth. "I always hated your side of the family." She said this not as an apology, but as a challenge. "Everyone was so oppressively normal. Uncle Carey with his nice respectable middle management job. Promotions and transfers from one upscale suburb to the next. Aunt Ellen the perfect corporate wife. And Garrett and Chrissie and Jan, the wünderkind."

Garrett looked troubled. "You sound so contemptuous. I mean, it's not as if we chose to be born into that kind of setting…"

"You want me to talk? Then shut up!" Gina ordered. "The issue of choice is immaterial here." She signaled to the waitress in a short red ruffled skirt to bring her another club soda. Garrett declined a third drink.

"You may be sorry," Gina warned. Then she continued, "On the other hand, there's my family. Do you know that my mother is an alcoholic?"

Garrett looked embarrassed, and his Southern-tinged accent deepened. "I don't think it's necessary to talk that way about your mother," he demurred.

"Necessary? It's the truth!" Gina exploded. Two businessmen at the bar turned around to look at her. "What're you lookin' at?" she growled in her best New York manner, and they hastily turned around.

Garrett pulled out a handkerchief and wiped at his forehead. This was starting to turn into something he might not be able to control. It seemed to make him nervous and excited at the same time.

"My mother," she lowered her voice only slightly, "has put away a pint of scotch every day since I can remember. But that's the least of it," she waved her hand in a gesture of dismissal. "Her first husband, who I refer to as my sperm donor – that being his singular contribution to my existence – is best left undiscussed. Her second husband was a professional gambler. Dear old Dave lost a total of three houses and seven automobiles in the six years she was married to him.

"Her third husband," Gina's voice grew brittle, "decided that he needed to teach his little thirteen-year-old step-daughter the facts of life, out in the garage. Those lessons were extensive and continued for a couple of years on a regular weekly basis."

Garrett broke in, outraged, "Did your mother know?"

"Know what?" Gina demanded. "Know that Dave bet and lost three houses and seven automobiles? Yeah, she knew. We had to move and take the bus a lot."

"Don't play games," he said sternly. "Did she know about… the other?"

"The other?" Gina mocked him. "What my mother knows and what she lets herself know are often two completely different stories." She dismissed this. "Just a few more facts, cousin. I'm giving you the Reader's Digest Condensed version, fit for family consumption. Don't worry, I'm not going to start describing everything I learned in the garage. Or tell you about how he threatened to kill me when I finally decided to leave home.

"Those things aren't very interesting anyway." She tipped her glass and took a long drink of club soda. "I'm an alcoholic too. I'm in AA now, that's why I don't drink anymore. And a cocaine addict. I've been off it about eight years, but I had a heavy habit. It makes you do a lot of not-very-nice things with a lot of not-very-nice people." She tossed her head in defiance. "There's more, but that's enough for now. You begin to see the gulf between us?"

"Jesus, Gina." Garrett was genuinely upset. "I don't even know what to say. I didn't have any idea about most of this. I'm just really shocked."

"Spare me the moral indignation." She flexed her palm in a "halt" gesture. "It kind'a makes me sick. What I find most interesting is how you could go through life and not know. Not have the faintest idea what was going on in your precious family." She snorted. "Now that's protection. That's privilege!"

Garrett's handsome face was a mess of disturbance. "Well, yes, that is a question," he said defensively, "but it's not like you or anybody else was talking about it. Nobody told us."

"Jesus Christ, it was there to see! It was right in front of your eyes!" Gina slammed her fist on the table, which made everyone in the bar go silent for a moment as they turned to check out the source of the uproar. A second later they resumed their quiet buzz, a little self-consciously, convinced after meeting Gina's eyes that they did not want to know what was going on.

"Let's forget it," Gina snapped. "It was a mistake to get into it in the first place. Now even you can understand that. So just put me on the plane and go home to your nice safe dull life and leave me the hell alone."

She was furious with herself. She'd wanted to shock her cousin awake, to make him see the reality behind his complacent middle-class life. The last thing she'd tolerate was for him to feel sorry for her.

"Shit, let's get out of here," she said roughly. "I shouldn't have even come here to see that crazy old bastard get buried."

"Gina, don't you care about anybody?" Garrett sounded bone weary.

"Whaddaya mean, care about anybody? What's that got to do with the price of lemons?"

"Well, you call your mother an alcoholic. You hate me cause I'm too normal. Now, Grandpa's a crazy old bastard." Garrett was losing it.

"Well, he was. Crazy, I mean. That's all I meant." Gina was off-handed. She didn't understand what was the big deal.

"What are you talking about? Grandpa wasn't crazy!" For the first time, he sounded angry.

"He sure as hell was. Don't tell me – God, you don't even know about that?" Gina was incredulous.

"Know what, Gina? Cut it out!"

She almost felt sorry for him. She'd been born without her innocence and had had thirty-one years to get used to it. Her poor cousin was losing his all in one afternoon.

She calmed down and looked him right in the eye, with what she hoped was a kind expression on her face. "Garrett, our grandfather was a manic-depressive. Ever since our mothers were kids. He was in and out of institutions, he had a shitload of shock treatments, and he was maintained on medication, that is, when he'd take it. Is this really all news to you?"

"I don't even know whether to believe it. I don't know if I believe anything you've said." He sounded sulky, like a child who's had something precious taken away and doesn't understand why.

She rubbed a hand over her face. "I can't believe Ellen kept this a secret," she said shaking her head. "I completely miscalculated this family's capacity for denial."

There was a long and awkward pause. Garrett stared into the remains of his drink while Gina let herself be distracted by the hockey game on the TV screen to one side of the bar.

When he spoke again, Garrett's voice was desolate. "I feel as if now I've really lost my grandfather. It's worse than when I heard he died." He started playing with the ketchup bottle on the table, spinning it around on its hard circular edge. "You know, I always felt so close to Grandpa. I used to be jealous of you because you spent so much time with him and Grandma."

"I got shipped off there whenever Mom and Dave were out of a place to live!" Gina interjected with a short gust of a laugh.

"You had your turn to talk. Now you've got to listen to me," Garrett insisted, and Gina settled back against the booth. "I didn't know why you were there. I always thought they invited you because there was only one of you and three of us. I used to ask if I could go ahead and visit them, during the summers, but my mother always had something else for me to do – golf lessons, or camp, or anything.

"So I only saw them on holidays when they'd come to visit, or we'd go there, and there always seemed to be such a large crowd. But Grandpa always came and talked to me, talked a lot about his life, or what was in the news, or what was on TV. He'd take me on these long walks and he always seemed to know everybody. I thought he was just so active and outgoing. I thought he was the most interesting guy in the world."

"Yeah, right. A guy who'd get up at five in the morning and spend the whole day out walking, talking to every stranger who would listen, or even to those who wouldn't. Yeah, he was active and outgoing alright." Gina leaned forward and put her elbows on the table. "So what did you think when he stopped talking and sat in a chair for the last fifteen years of his life?"

"I thought it was his stroke." His voice was plaintive.

She nodded thoughtfully.

"Why would my mother keep that a secret from all of us? " he demanded to know.

Gina waved one hand dismissively. "Don't waste one minute trying to figure out the why of anything. It'll make you crazy."

Seeing that he would not let go of it that easily, she tried again. "Look at it this way. Grandpa had two kids – my mom and your mom. My mom gets drunk and acts out and marries the wrong men and is extreme in every way. Your mom does everything she's supposed to do and keeps her mouth shut." Gina shrugged. "They're Grandpa's children."

Garrett nodded eagerly. This was an answer to why, an explanation he could wrap his rationality around.

"Yes, and they produced us!" he announced.

"Exactly."

They were quiet again for a minute or two. Then Gina said, "So I guess you never heard the story about how Grandpa's family died?"

He sighed and put his head in his hands.

"Do you want to?" she asked, aware that he might have had enough reality for one night.

"Why not? Why have any illusions left?" he replied with some bitterness.

"Now you sound like me. I only bring it up because I always heard my mother say it was the thing that sent Grandpa over the edge. Even though the science people now say that manic-depression is all chemical."

"Go ahead. Tell me."

"As my mother tells it, she and your mom were about ten, eleven, twelve, somewhere in there. Grandpa had gone on a trip, to Illinois, well, here, to see his family. His dad was already dead of something. I forget what."

Gina was suddenly cold. She shivered and pulled her leather jacket closer around her. "So I guess it was a night sorta like this – a miserable bastard of a snowstorm – and they were out on the highway. It was Grandpa and his mother and his sister Ellen – your mom's named after her – and somebody else. His aunt maybe? I forget."

"Go on!" he urged impatiently.

"You could almost tell the rest of the story yourself. It was a blinding snowstorm. They're in this car out on this country road. Maybe they're on their way home from church or something. I don't know. Grandpa's mother was driving – I guess she always insisted on driving. They never saw the truck."

Gina stopped then because she saw Garrett wiping tears out of his eyes. "Hey, it was a long time ago," she said softly.

"I know." He tried to control his shoulders, which were shaking with sobs. "Go ahead."

"Well, everybody died horribly. Except Grandpa. His mother was decapitated. His sister ..." She saw the expression on his face, his horror at both the details and her emotionless recitation of them. "Well, I guess it was pretty brutal. Grandpa was thrown clear out of the car and into a snowdrift. Almost no injuries."

"He survived and nobody else did. How could he explain it to himself?" Garrett wondered aloud.

"Mom says it wasn't a year after that that he went into the hospital for the first time."

"God! I never knew any of it. I just thought Grandpa was a really happy guy." His voice was low with self-contempt. He looked at Gina and asked simply, "Do you think you could hold my hand for a minute?"

Without comment she reached across the table and took his smooth hand into both of hers. They sat in companionable silence as the Maple Leafs scored a goal and the bar erupted in half-hearted groans.

"Thank you," he said after some time had passed. He seemed somewhat more composed.

Still she kept holding his hand.

"I don't know what to do," Garrett implored. "Do you think I should confront my mother about this?"

Gina grimaced at him. "I confront my mother every time I breathe. She just can't figure out why I didn't turn out more like you!" They both laughed, but then she turned serious. "Ellen's figured out a way to get through her life. It's not my way, but it works for her. Is there anything for you to gain by trying to change that?"

"I don't know. Maybe you're right."

They lapsed into silence once more.

Finally Gina looked at her watch and said, "I should get a move on here. It'll take me a while to return the car."

"Don't you want to call and see if your plane's been delayed again?" he suggested.

She shook her head. "What difference would it make? I'm not going back to town no matter what. I'll spend the night in the airport if I have to. I'll drink coffee, play video games. It'll be fine. I like airports. They're so impersonal."

He grinned at her. "You always do the extreme thing, don't you?"

"Nope. Just most of the time. Like you're not always careful and moderate."

Garrett was willing to be teased. "Just most of the time."

She stood then, ignoring the businessman at the next table who turned to gawk at her short leather skirt. She pulled on an oversized men's wool coat. Garrett reluctantly took her cue and stood too, throwing some bills on the table.

They reached the entryway and waited while Garrett put on his gloves and wrapped a muffler around his neck. She dug her bare hands deep into the pockets of her coat. She was amused but cooperative when he held the door open for her.

They stepped out into a thick swirl of snow, illuminated against the black sky by the halogen lights of the parking lot. The freeway hummed along just beside them. They hugged briefly in their bulky coats.

"I really want to thank you for coming," Garrett said with emotion.

Gina replied lightly, "Thanks for the ticket."

He started to say something else, but she reached out and touched her index finger to his lips. "See ya'," she said.

He turned and began walking toward his car. She watched him for a moment, admiring the slope of his shoulders, his athletic gait.

On impulse she reached into her bag and rummaged until she found her camera. She had thought to bring it along at the last minute but hadn't taken it out of its case until just now. She unscrewed the lens cap and brought it up to her eye.

"Garrett!" she called, and he spun around. For a moment he looked unlike himself, instead like a dark wild bird about to rush toward her, snow flying all around him. Quickly she pressed the shutter.

garage sale

"Don't you ever let me do that again!" Cassandra moaned. Her head was bent over as she marked prices on little tags and affixed them to the merchandise displayed on the front lawn.

"Do what?" I hadn't really been listening. Cassandra could go on and on. I was trying to decide whether I really wanted to part with those black and yellow cowboy boots I'd found years ago in a "free" box. They just needed new heels and a bit of shine.

"Fall in love with someone who hates cats!" Cassandra proclaimed in a voice that could be heard down the block. "I should have known it was the sign of a dysfunctional personality."

I stared over at her three cats – Felicia, a long-haired orange tabby; Marcus Welby, a sleek black hunter; and Albino, an all-white cat who'd been diagnosed with leukemia years ago, but was none the worse for wear. All three were stretched out the full-length of a chaise lounge, working on their tans, no doubt.

Indirectly it was these three who were responsible for this garage sale. The sale, which Cassandra had roped me into doing with her, was being held because Cassandra was moving out of the house on Birch Street. She was moving out because she and Gerald, her boyfriend of three years, were breaking up. It's not that they lived together; Gerald wouldn't live there because of the cats. But Cassandra insisted, "There are too many memories. I have to put this behind me."

Gerald and Cassandra had a million reasons for breaking up. As near as I could tell, and I've been Cassandra's best friend ever since we met in group therapy years ago, their relationship had been little more than a three-year break-up. Never had I seen two people more incompatible.

Cassandra made her living, such as it was, as an astrologer and tarot card reader. She approached these practices with utter seriousness and relentlessly subdued skeptics with tales of accurate predictions. She was overly fond of the color purple – the house on Birch Street was entirely decorated in shades of it – and adored cats. She claimed the ability to communicate with them psychically.

Gerald was a stockbroker, or maybe he was an investment banker. I never could figure out exactly what Gerald did, but it had something to do with finances. Although a young man, not yet thirty when Cassandra met him, he dressed more conservatively than my father. There was a starched, buttoned-down feel to his whole personality. Gerald was rational. Gerald was scientific. Gerald was allergic to cats.

"What would you pay for this?" Cassandra interrupted my thoughts and held up a globe of the night sky that lit from the inside.

"Nothing," I said. "I don't want a globe of the night sky."

"Don't be exasperating! Imagine if you did."

"Uhh, a dollar?" I offered dubiously. She gave up on me and scribbled something on the tag.

I think they met in a bar. She was going out to a lot of bars in those days. This was at a time when Cassandra's horoscope kept predicting that she was destined to meet someone. Whenever we went out together, she'd be craning her neck the whole time, scanning all around the room to see if this was it. I wasn't with her the night she met Gerald. Even now it's hard for me to imagine what straight buttoned-down Gerald and Madame Cassandra saw in each other. They say opposites attract, but this was ridiculous.

If it sounds like I don't like Gerald, I have to admit it's true. Gerald could never understand why Cassandra, who's as heterosexual as they come, would want to hang out with someone like me. A lesbian. *A deviant.* He actually called me that; I couldn't believe it.

So there was no love lost between Gerald and me. But all during the last three years I really made an effort to mind my own business. Which wasn't easy, because hardly a day went by that Cassandra didn't call me up to complain about Gerald, or to tell me that he had broken up with her once again.

Each of them had a lengthy list of complaints. His included that she dressed like a hippie, that she ate only rabbit food, that her house was untidy, that her friends were losers and deviants, that she was hopeless with managing her money, that her profession was disreputable, and that she was too noisy when she had orgasms. Her list contained such grievances as: he's a carnivore, he watches too much TV, his friends are boring and uptight, he's never done drugs, he's an unadventurous lover.

One might wonder, why did Cassandra persist? I certainly had reason to ask that question plenty of times. Cassandra claimed to believe that they were astrologically fated, their destinies twined together by the alignment of the planets. In the first place they'd met when Venus and Jupiter were conjunct in her seventh house, she explained to me. After knowing Cassandra all these years, these terms have a ring of familiarity, even though I couldn't tell you exactly what they mean. Not only that, his moon was trined to hers, and both of them had Mars in Sagittarius. These facts convinced her, beyond all reason, beyond sanity, in my opinion, that Gerald was her one true soul mate.

I don't know what Gerald's excuse was. Maybe she offered him an escape from that precise little world of suits and numbers. You know, a walk on the wild side? Maybe all the chaos and upheaval got his blood going. Cassandra claimed that despite his complaints he was crazy about her in bed. One can never really tell about these things.

The cats took the brunt of it. Felicia, Marcus Welby, and Albino became the battleground over which Gerald and Cassandra pitched their relationship. Gerald perceived, and correctly I'm sure, that Cassandra loved these fur-covered creatures in a way that she never loved him. They came to symbolize everything that he found fault with in Cassandra.

One thing I'll say about cats, they have an infallible sixth sense. They can spot a cat-hater or an allergic at a hundred paces. Cassandra's felines were wise to Gerald from the first day she brought him home. They didn't wait for him to start sneezing to carpet his crisp Navy blue suit with orange and white hairs. They did wait until Gerald and Cassandra were sleeping, then crept stealthily into bed and arranged themselves on all sides of Gerald's pillow.

Gerald would wake up wheezing and toss the cats one by one off the side of the bed. According to Cassandra, those "tosses" became more like touchdown passes as time went on. She would berate him for animal abuse and threaten to call the SPCA. Gerald would gasp that he'd be sending her the cleaning bill for his suits.

In all fairness, I have to admit that Cassandra didn't help things any. She wouldn't hear of keeping the cats outside when Gerald was over; after all, it was their home too. Cassandra insisted that allergies were all in the mind, and that Gerald could cure himself once he learned to embrace his own animal nature. She set for herself the task of helping him do that, and took to draping her body in leopard skin underwear instead of taking the practical steps that might have done some good, like vacuuming the carpet or laundering the pillowcases more frequently.

Gerald, Cassandra, and the cats became a textbook study of the Havelock Triangle – you know, Victim/Rescuer/Persecutor? Cassandra would try to be nice and keep the cats out of the bedroom for a night. One of them would retaliate by vomiting a hairball into Gerald's shiny black Cole/Hahn loafers. Gerald would discover this as he was rushing out to a meeting with an important client, and scream at Cassandra that she was slovenly and out-of-control. He'd threaten to punish the cats. Cassandra would pick one up and nuzzle it for protection and comfort.

Cassandra entertained me with stories like this on a daily basis. I'd learned years before not to say much. Most people want sympathy, not advice, and even if they say they want counsel, they ignore it and go on and do whatever it is they were going to do anyway. Besides, I didn't like Gerald. It's not that I ever told that to Cassandra, I'd mostly just sit on the other end of the phone or across the table in her kitchen and nod and murmur sympathetically. But I certainly wasn't about to take his part.

Aside from telling Cassandra on more than one occasion that her friends – meaning me – were deviants, here's how Gerald got on my shit list. Cassandra had called one day and asked if I'd come over and help her fix the leaking shower head in her bathtub. Help her really meant would I do it, because Cassandra and the world of mechanical repair do not exist in the same time/space continuum. I said sure. It so happened I was taking a sick day off of work – I'm an installer for the phone company, one of the first women in my district. So anyway, I went over there, and fixed the shower head.

It was a hot day, one of those days when I was grateful not to be crawling around under somebody's house looking for a cable, and I was pretty sweaty by the time I was done. So Cassandra says, why don't you take a shower and cool off. This seemed like a good idea, and afterwards she loaned me this terrycloth robe to put on and sit around in for awhile. Turns out the robe is Gerald's. So I'm sitting there in the living room in this navy blue robe, with my bare feet propped up on the coffee table, having a beer with Cassandra, and all of a sudden Gerald comes in. And right away, before anybody can say a word, he gets bug-eyed. He wants to know what this deviant is doing sitting in Cassandra's living room with no clothes on wearing his bathrobe.

Well, Cassandra thinks it's hysterical and starts to laugh, but I guess I'm not a very patient person when it comes to some things. I stood up and got right in his face – I'm an inch shorter than Gerald, but way more muscular, from climbing those poles. I can't remember exactly how I put it but it was something to the effect that I'd been friends with Cassandra since before he ever got his MBA, and that if I wanted to sleep with her and she wanted it too there'd be nothing he could do to stop it, but it so happened that I didn't and she didn't either, so he should just chill the hell out.

Cassandra didn't stand up for me quite like I would've liked her to. She was busy telling him how ridiculous it was, she's as heterosexual as Eve, or something. But it was easier to be mad at him than at her. After that I made it a point never to be over there when he was around.

The denouement for Cassandra and Gerald came about a month ago when Marcus Welby broke an irreplaceable Ming vase that had belonged to Gerald's mother. He'd given it to Cassandra either during one of the rare times when he was feeling optimistic about the two of them, or during one of the frequent times when he was on a campaign to improve her, I forget which.

Gerald was arguing with Cassandra about how she needed to change the cat litter more frequently. One of the reasons, he said, that the cats were disgusting was because Cassandra took such disgustingly bad care of them. Somehow during the melee Marcus Welby climbed up on top of this high bookcase, where even Cassandra didn't allow those cats to go, and with one good swat made debris out of that vase.

For Gerald it was the last straw. He told Cassandra that the next chance he had he was going to take those three demons from hell on a long long drive. When Cassandra got home she wouldn't know what happened to them, nobody would, but she'd never see them again. Well, that was it for Cassandra. You can call her a slob, insult her oldest friend, you can even be a boring lover. But don't threaten to disappear her cats.

Later she told me, "And to think, if it wasn't for Marcus Welby, I might never have seen his true nature!"

That was the last of Gerald. Cassandra and the cats were moving to a little guesthouse in Silver Lake. The lawn in front of the Birch Street house was littered with dispossessed items, a large number of them purple.

On the chaise lounge, the cats were taking it all in stride. Felicia was curled up behind Albino, cleaning his ears with her tongue. Every now and then his white tail would flick back and forth with pleasure. Marcus Welby rolled over onto his back to take a long deep stretch.

"The best part," Cassandra called to me across a table where she was arranging an assortment of leopard skin underwear, "is that Uranus is finally leaving my seventh house! Now maybe I can find a stable relationship."

"I don't think they come any more stable than Gerald," I told her. "Maybe you should be careful what you ask for. Whaddaya think, Cassandra, should I keep these cowboy boots or what?"

"Keep them," she said, with no hesitation, "or you'll be sorry later." It was the same tone she used on her clients when she read the stars to predict their futures.

what annie said

Madeleine woke up that morning knowing that today she was going to leave. It wasn't anything she had been conscious of deciding, say, the night before or even in a dream. It was as if the thought had risen as the moon set, and she woke knowing it with certainty.

She'd hadn't known she'd been thinking about leaving. There'd been no prolonged struggle, no weighing of options or consequences. But somewhere Madeleine must have been thinking about it all along, a low hum she'd been hearing for a long time but only just now begun to listen to.

Madeleine woke before the fog had cleared. The filtered gray light in the room lent an aura of protection, the damp chilly air gave her clarity. Her eyes traveled about the room, its bare white walls and prim furnishings. They lingered over each detail, memorizing, saying good-bye.

She sat up and stretched back the white sheet in a wide arc, revealing a body grown new, strong and full of purpose. She felt an appreciation for her muscles, lean and ready for work to do. They would carry her out of this house and down some street she didn't yet know the name of.

Still seated on the edge of the bed, she reached behind her and quickly wound her dark hair into a simple braid that ribboned down her spine. Madeleine felt an urgency to attend to business, to accomplish what was in front of her without the burdens of doubt or sentiment.

She went first into the small bathroom that adjoined her room and without turning on the overhead lamp, began to stare at herself in the scarred mirror over the sink. The dark eyes which gazed back held no questions, only deep wells of light. Her features were calm, it seemed that even the lines that had begun to define themselves around her eyes and mouth had receded.

Bending, Madeleine hastily splashed some water over her face and raised her eyes again to her image, watching as drops glided down her cheeks to land on her breasts. She smiled at the woman before her, whose face shone with water, whose breasts glittered with drops.

There were sounds coming from another part of the house, but Madeleine was unconcerned. For the first time it seemed that this activity had nothing to do with her. It had never occurred to her that she could simply leave, though now she couldn't imagine why not.

She pulled a rough towel to her face and rubbed vigorously. The face that emerged was reddened. Madeleine ignored the lotions and oils that spread along the shelf beneath the mirror. She by-passed the little pile atop the cabinet by the sink, where her rings and watch had been resting since the night before. She left the bathroom.

With the covers thrown back the bed looked like an open wound. It still bore the imprint of her body. She hid the evidence by pulling the spread up to the head of the bed, smoothing the pillows and laying them neatly on top.

The motion disturbed Emerson, the black and white spotted tom who liked to sleep between the pillows. Momentarily her heart caught as the cat stretched and looked her expectantly. Madeleine reached down, enfolded her hands underneath his belly and scooped him up into her arms like an infant. She hugged him tight and put her nose in his ear, then whispered something into his soft fur.

She let him go and he jumped to the windowsill to watch the unfolding of the day. From her closet Madeleine pulled a simple blue dress and slipped it over her head, letting it fall across her small breasts and narrow hips, feeling the hem swoosh against her calves. She chose the dress for this reason: nothing exceptional had ever happened to her in it. No one had given it to her; it wasn't her favorite color; she had neither bought it nor worn it to celebrate any kind of occasion.

Disregarding stockings she slipped her feet into a pair of huaraches, comfortably worn but still holding up. Briefly she considered a coat which had cost quite a lot of money very recently, but she chose instead a pale yellow sweater that had belonged to her mother, and wrapped it around her shoulders against the morning chill.

That was it. She was ready. She picked up her wallet and dropped it into a pocket in the blue dress. Her purse and keys she left on the low bureau. At the door Madeleine paused to look again at the room, at the view from its windows, the sun attempting to disperse the fog. She felt a cool emptiness inside this space.

As she opened the door Emerson followed her into the hall. She walked noiselessly past Russ' door, grateful to find it still closed. She could presume that her husband was still asleep. From the wide-open door of the boys' room she deduced that they were already up and gone somewhere. Madeleine felt relief. She wanted neither to sneak nor to argue. She wanted not to rush and not to be delayed.

Emerson led the way down the staircase, trotting ahead but pausing often to look back, to make sure she still followed. At the bottom of the stairs he continued in the direction of the kitchen, but she veered off toward the front door. Dismayed, he cried in protest, a sharp howl, and she quickly turned toward the kitchen to hush him.

"Mama?"

In the kitchen Madeleine was confronted by the sight of Annie, her youngest. The child sat in the breakfast nook, still in her striped pink pajamas, surrounded by boxes of cereal – she liked to mix them – and watching cartoons with the sound turned off. Her bare feet swung rhythmically against the wood of the bench.

"Mama?" Annie asked again, this time turning around to look as her mother poured crunchies into the cat dish.

Madeleine did not trust herself to speak. She felt suddenly that if she opened her mouth, if she said even one simple word to her daughter, the spell of the morning would break and she'd stay forever. Instead she walked over the kissed the top of the girl's head. Annie's dark hair was short and tousled, sticking out all over in crazy spikes. Madeleine held back the impulse to smooth it. Annie was eight now and was beginning to claim autonomy over her lithe body.

Annie put down her spoon and reached for her mother. Madeleine grasped the small hand and felt the stickiness of sugar and milk. Scooting over on the bench Annie made room for Madeleine to sit down. Reluctantly she did.

There were many mornings when Annie might ask for this kind of time, but Madeleine was usually unable to give it, busy with chores and routine, her time and attention fragmented between Russ and the steady roar the boys always made when they were home. She often felt that she saw Annie on the periphery of her vision.

Today there were none of the distractions, no schedule to attend to. Time had contorted and assumed a form quite unlike its usual shape. Russ would sleep on forever, the boys would remain out wherever they were, nothing would happen, Madeleine felt certain, as long as she sat here with Annie.

"I had a dream, Mama."

Madeleine used her arms to scoop her daughter into her lap, half-expecting her to protest, but Annie yielded easily. She stared up into her mother's face with eyes that were intense and dark.

"At first I was on the playground, all by myself. I had my ballerina dress on and I was dancing and dancing, but nobody was there to look at me."

She halted her discourse, momentarily distracted by the images on the screen, three muscle-y looking cartoon figures chasing a blonde boy into a cave. She absent-mindedly took another spoonful of cereal, but it was soggy by that time and she spilled it back into the bowl. Looking back up at her mother, Annie resumed.

"Then I was in a forest, wait, I think so, there were all these trees. And I walked and walked. I was all by myself again. Then I saw you. Only, you were really little, smaller than me. Like the size of Petunia."

Petunia was her doll, her favorite since she was four or five. Though Annie didn't play much with dolls anymore, she always asked for Petunia when she was sick or sad.

"You were inside this glass bowl, like a cage. It was just a little bigger than you were and it was like a playhouse. But you were sad, Mama, you were crying." She stopped again, to search her mother's face for a response.

Madeleine kept holding her, though the arm Annie leaned against had gone to sleep. She tried to imagine what Annie saw as she looked into her eyes. Then she knew, ruefully, that Annie was telling her everything she saw, in the language of the dream.

"I wanted to ask Daddy what to do, but I couldn't find him. So I picked up the bowl of glass. I thought maybe you'd come and play with me. But you ran away, really fast. I tried to run after you. I called to you but you didn't stop. Then you were gone." Annie's hands gripped tighter around her neck.

"Then what happened?" Madeleine was surprised to hear her own voice. It sounded as though her throat were full of sand.

"I woke up then. I didn't want to go back to sleep. It was a bad dream." She sighed and curled her dark head into Madeleine's shoulder.

The warmth of the girl's breath on her neck sank Madeleine's heart. She stroked Annie's hair and marveled at the dream. Was her daughter a witch, with her deep eyes that could see what was really there?

Madeleine found that she wasn't concerned about the others. Only this little witch girl, dozing in her lap. She felt her stomach roll over, like a giant wave. She knew that time would not suspend itself forever. In a few minutes, the boys would bang through the kitchen door, or Russ would come padding down the stairs singing a snatch of an old Sinatra song. Then the glass bowl would be safely in place once again.

Gently she stirred Annie, who obediently rolled off Madeleine's lap, plunking her bare feet down on the linoleum. Madeleine stood up too, but right away knelt down before her daughter.

In the voice of sand she whispered, "Your dreams can't hurt you. Pay attention. They'll tell you things." She looked deep into Annie's eyes, and the girl nodded as though she understood. Madeleine took one more moment to give her a long hug, and kissed the top of her head. Then she released her, and Annie scampered out of the kitchen and up the stairs.

lifelong

After Fran died, Carolyn's friends all told her to get Fran's things cleared out of the house as quickly as she could. They'd barely been home from the cemetery an hour, had scarcely finished setting out the platters of cold chicken and sliced roast beef, bowls of carrot-raisin and potato salads, loaves of bread and tins of brownies on the dining room table, the one Fran had spent all winter building twenty years ago, before the assembled intimates began giving Carolyn advice.

"I'll come over early next week and help you box things up and take them over to the thrift shop," Irene announced. She looked funny, bustling around the kitchen in a wool skirt that stretched tight over her broad girth. Her legs seemed naked in nylon stockings in a way they never did in shorts. Somehow she'd been delegated the task of making the coffee, though everyone knew Irene always brewed it thick as mud.

"That's a good idea," Jean affirmed in the Southern drawl she'd never managed to shake. She was busy dabbing at a spot of mustard that had slid from her sandwich onto the front of her good white shirt. "Better to do it fast and get it over with."

"You've got to make a new life for yourself," Peg declared in a tone at once bossy and solicitous. She tossed her sleek blonde pageboy. "That's what Fran would want."

Carolyn believed, but did not say, that what Fran would want was to still be here with Carolyn in the old life they had shared for thirty-two-and-a-half years. She could imagine Fran circling the dining room table, piling her plate high with her friends' cooking, the way she always did, at Peg's annual Fourth of July barbecue, at Lois's traditional New Year's Eve bash. Fran would have easily dispensed with their unsolicited wisdom, saying, "Now, don't poke your nose in where it doesn't belong," firmly, but without a trace of rancor.

Carolyn wasn't quite able to manage that; instead she'd ducked beneath her friends' well-meaning words, neither agreeing nor protesting, as if the swell of counsel were a giant wave breaking over her. She hoped that, when she surfaced, the women would all be gone and she could go lie down alone in the bed where she and Fran had slept since they were both young women, the bed in which Fran had died only three days ago. Carolyn wanted to lie there in the dark, smelling whatever traces of Fran remained, drawing them deep inside where they could not be taken away.

It wasn't that Carolyn didn't love their friends, women she and Fran had known for decades, had in fact grown up and grown old with. She owed them debts she could never begin to repay. Lois had come every day to read to Fran during the long, awful siege of chemotherapy, her voice patient and melodious. Jean was the one who'd driven them home the day the doctor had told Fran, "There's nothing more we can do," and had stoically held back her own tears in order to comfort Carolyn.

Peg had sat with Fran for hours going over bank statements and legal documents, taking care of unresolved business. Irene had been the one to call the others, the night she'd heard from Carolyn that Fran was gone. Without their devoted attention, their resolve and practicality, Carolyn couldn't imagine how she would have gotten through these last ten months. Even now her house was cleaned, her refrigerator bursting with food, due to the ministrations of these women.

Still, it was pure relief to close the door on the last of them, finicky Evelyn, whom Carolyn found scouring the stove top with a copper Chore Boy. Evelyn had always gotten on Fran's nerves, and Carolyn knew Fran would not have had any qualms about saying, "Evelyn, just stop that. It's time to go home." Carolyn had never been blunt with people; it was not her way. She was the kind of woman who would rather be put out herself than inconvenience another. She gently approached Evelyn and said bashfully, "I think it's clean enough."

Evelyn, who always took even the gentlest correction as a severe rebuke, grew flustered. "Oh, I'm sorry, I just thought I'd help out." Her wheedling tone made Carolyn feel guilty to have spoken, but, remembering Fran, she said, "Thanks so much. I'm just a little tired now," and Evelyn scuttled away.

Tired she was. Carolyn had taken to sitting up beside Fran at night for the last few weeks, dozing but alert to every shift in Fran's breathing, every moan or movement. The last two nights, ever since Fran had been bundled into a plastic bag and carried away, Carolyn had simply wandered the house, a stranger to the rooms they'd occupied for nearly three decades.

She felt suddenly as if every ounce of energy had been sucked from her sixty-year-old body, a gas tank drained of even the fumes, nothing left to fuel her. Fran had always followed an elaborate ritual of closing up the house for the night, checking the locks on the doors and windows, shutting off the lamps and switching on nightlights. Even at her sickest she'd pestered Carolyn to follow the routine, rasping from her bed, "Don't forget to check the basement latch," and Carolyn had faithfully obliged. Tonight, though, Carolyn hadn't the stamina. She couldn't quite recall if she'd locked the front door behind Evelyn, but neither could she bring herself to check it.

Guiltily, she collapsed onto the bed without even removing her clothes. Lois had tried yesterday to change the sheets, but Carolyn had diverted her by asking her to drive to the airport to pick up the cousin of Fran's who'd flown in for the service. "You can't leave those on there," Lois objected, waving her delicate hands. "She was so ill." But Carolyn had retorted, "It was cancer, Lois, I'm not going to catch it." The sickness and the drugs and the process of dying had all changed Fran's scent, from salty and robust into something softer, sweet and pungent, the aroma of decay, but even this now was dear to Carolyn. She hugged Fran's pillow to her chest and inhaled. It was not like having Fran there with her, but it was like having a memory.

○

On Monday morning of the following week, Irene arrived at eight in her van; Peg was right behind her in her BMW convertible. Both vehicles were laden with empty cartons, carefully preserved in closets and attics for just such an occasion. Watching them confer in her driveway, Carolyn was transported back years to when Irene had helped Fran and Carolyn move into this house, back when they were young. Irene had owned a truck then, a Ford, a red one, in which she took a lot of pride. Then as now, she was a big woman, athletic, and she was always being called upon to help move the women in their circle.

It had been a hot day, September; they'd started early in the morning and by mid-afternoon were sitting around with cold beers in what had then been the scruffy, untended backyard. Jean had come over later to help unpack, her nurse's uniform exchanged for dungarees, and had immediately begun instructing Carolyn in what she ought to do to fix up the yard ("I'd pull out those ratty-looking shrubs and get a flowerbed going along the garage. And if you plant a citrus tree there in the back, in a few years you'll have fruit and shade!") To this day, Carolyn enjoyed the Meyer lemons she plucked from that tree.

Peg was the agent who'd sold them the house, and when she stopped by later that night with a casserole dish and a bottle of wine to check on how they were settling in, she'd been only too happy to pour a glass and join the other women, her high heels making little holes in the dirt of the backyard. They hadn't even known Lois then, Carolyn recalled, but met her not too long after that.

Now Carolyn waited until the doorbell rang to open the door, less happy than she wanted to be to see their kind, determined faces. Irene had retired from teaching high school geometry two years earlier, and was dressed as she now was most days, in a relaxed pair of cotton slacks and a tidy, oversize T-shirt that hugged an ample torso. Today's T-shirt bore the logo of the senior women's softball team for which she pitched. Although she scarcely needed the money, Peg still kept her hand in real estate, and her tailored linen suit signaled that she had clients scheduled for later that day. Carolyn greeted them with hugs, assuring the two that she'd been sleeping just fine, waving away Peg's offer of a few Xanax.

"I've got the van cleared out and we're ready to haul," Irene announced, but Carolyn balked.

"I'm don't think I'm quite ready to do that," she said meekly, looking away from them at the view outside the kitchen window.

"I don't think you oughta drag your feet on this," Peg protested, dropping her trim leather handbag onto the kitchen counter. "The longer you put it off, the more painful it's going to be."

Ordinarily this group could bully Carolyn into almost anything. Not that they were cruel or mean-spirited; they were simply women with forcefully held opinions, and they certainly seemed to know more of the world than she did. Over the years they'd persuaded her to go camping in the High Sierras (where she'd gotten altitude sickness and had to be carried down the mountain on the back of a mule), to drink Margaritas in Oaxaca (and she had gotten violently ill, just as she'd predicted), to invest in a mutual fund (which had turned a handsome profit), and to sell her 1966 Mustang, something she still regretted having done.

Carolyn would often look to Fran for counsel in these circumstances. Fran always seemed able to make up her own mind and once she had, nothing anyone could say would sway her. Only Peg had the temerity to really contradict her, but Fran had a way of holding her ground and making it look effortless. Fran had never tried to influence Carolyn in her decisions, though. Always, when asked for her opinion, she would declare, "Whatever you want to do is okay by me."

Carolyn raised her chin in that stubborn way Fran used to. This time she met their eyes and said again, "I'm not ready. I appreciate all your help, but I have to take this at my own pace."

Peg and Irene exchanged glances. "It's not going to do you any good to put this off..." Peg started to argue, but Irene cut her off.

"That's OK, honey," Irene soothed in a jocular tone, running a meaty hand through her wild gray hair. "You just take your time. We don't mean to come in here like gangbusters and tell you what to do. Just let us know when you're ready, and we'll be here to help."

As the two women backed out of the door, Carolyn knew that within the hour everyone in their small circle would be informed of this development. Peg would no more than have backed out the driveway before she'd be on her cellular phone to Lois and then perhaps to Evelyn. Irene would drop by Jean's condo on the way home and pry her attention from the soaps. Amongst the five of them, plans would be suggested and discarded, strategies outlined and refined, all aimed at tackling the problem of Carolyn.

Once they were gone, it seemed more possible to hold on to the feeling of Fran. Carolyn ambled into the living room and sank onto the flowered couch. She was unaccustomed to having nothing to do; she'd only taken her retirement from the phone company once Fran started getting sick, and since that time she'd had her hands full with Fran's treatments and finally, with her dying. Although both Lois and Evelyn had lectured Carolyn about the importance of keeping busy, at this moment she was grateful for her leisure, grateful to have nothing more to do than to sit in her living room and listen to the birdsong beyond the window.

Her eyes strayed over the familiar objects in the living room, the worn recliner draped with a plaid blanket, a basket of shells collected from some long-ago Florida vacation. On the mantle above the fireplace was a framed photograph of herself and Fran, taken thirty-two years before. Carolyn rose to retrieve the photo, carrying it back to the couch. She studied the young faces that stared up at her, so fearless and unknowing. In the snapshot, Fran sported a short thatch of hair that had not changed substantially in style from that time to a few days ago, only its carroty color, which had first dimmed, then paled to white over the progression of years. Carolyn's own hair had been long then, an unimpressive shade of brown, but she had cut it no more than a year after this photo was taken, and worn it short ever since.

When she met Fran she'd been twenty-eight and already destined, seemingly, to be an old maid. Most of her friends had married right out of high school, but boys had never shown much interest in Carolyn. This would not have seemed cataclysmic to her had it not been so distressing to her mother, who regularly predicted that Carolyn would end up alone and bitter. At the age of twenty, Carolyn had taken a job at the phone company, where she'd received regular promotions until she was making enough to move out of her mother's home and get her own apartment. She liked living on her own, but it did get lonely, so when some of the women in her department started a bowling team, she'd gratefully agreed to join.

The married women on the team were eager to have a night away from their husbands, and the single ones were hoping to meet men. Only Carolyn was genuinely interested in bowling, and she grew impatient with the way the game lagged while her teammates flirted or gossiped about the men they'd left at home.

Fran had been on a team that bowled on the same night as Carolyn's. Carolyn had noticed her, and admired the little shake of the head she always gave when she bowled a strike, as if to deny any pride in her accomplishment. Although Carolyn didn't remember it when she was introduced to them later, both Irene and Jean were on that team with Fran as well.

They'd only met because one of Carolyn's teammates, a peroxide blonde whose name Carolyn could no longer remember, had gone off with a man she'd met in the bar and stranded Carolyn without a ride home.

"You don't mind, do ya', hon? Something real important just came up!" The woman had given a lopsided wink from beneath her white bangs, as if, of course, Carolyn would understand and share her priorities.

Carolyn was asking the man behind the counter about bus schedules when Fran walked up. "I couldn't help but overhear that you got stuck here. If you want, I could give you a ride home."

Something about the even gaze of Fran's blue eyes, the straightforward way in which she spoke, made Carolyn forget to be shy and she was glad to accept the offer. Just before Fran had dropped her off at the apartment, she'd asked Carolyn if she'd like to go to dinner the following night, and again Carolyn had said yes. She had no words in her vocabulary for the kind of woman Fran was, indeed, the kind of woman Carolyn was herself, but she had felt a sense of comfort and trust in Fran's presence that she never thought to question.

Years later she would ask Fran how she could have known about Carolyn, what trait or sign had clued her that Carolyn could be approached. Fran would shrug, insist there was no signal, no set of characteristics. She'd point to Peg, who had her blond hair done every week and always wore skirts and high heels, or to Evelyn, who'd been married and raised two children. "I saw you watching me," she finally explained, "and just thought I'd take a chance."

Carolyn knew there must have been some gossip at work when she started seeing Fran regularly, but nobody said anything to her face. The office bowling team disbanded after just one season, but by then she'd met Irene and Jean and others, a tightly knit network of friends who played sports, went to the movies, took vacations, and shot pool together in a tiny, dark bar on a side street in Hollywood. Her mother had been glad to see she'd finally had a "friend," but had never relented in her disappointment that her daughter had remained unwed.

The photo she now held in her hands had been taken by Jean at a picnic, perhaps a month after Fran drove Carolyn home from the bowling alley. It was a Sunday afternoon, one of those glorious February days in Southern California where the temperature soars to bring a foretaste of summer. What she remembered most about the day was that it was the first time Fran had kissed her.

"Come take a walk with me," Fran had encouraged, almost as soon as the group has pitched their blankets and arranged their baskets and coolers.

"Hey, where're you going with my first basewoman?" Irene hollered after them. She was trying to organize a little softball, but Fran advised her to start without them.

Fran had a sure, confidant stride that, on a man, might be called a swagger, but Fran never appeared cocky or boastful. She seemed to know the trail that led them deeper into a stand of trees, and there she kissed Carolyn without apology. All of Carolyn's mother's predictions of a lonely future melted away in those prolonged kisses.

A while later they made their way back, and the women greeted them with knowing grins, and Jean had snapped the picture. There was gentle teasing, which made Carolyn blush, and Fran say, "Don't you women have anything better to do?" Still, no one on that day, not even Fran and Carolyn, could have predicted that their bond would be lifelong.

It was a couple of months after the picnic when Carolyn learned that Fran and Jean had once been in love. They were out on a Friday night, shooting pool, drinking a couple of beers. Fran was showing Carolyn how to bank, her arms around Carolyn as she guided the cue. From the other end of the table Jean drawled, "I remember when you gave me that lesson!" She gave a broad wink to the others and the unflappable Fran had actually blushed.

"It was five years ago, it doesn't mean anything," Fran had insisted in the bar's tiny bathroom, while Carolyn had sobbed from inside the stall, "But you see her all the time. Isn't that because you're still in love with her?" Only the passage of time had convinced Carolyn that the bond between Fran and Jean was one of deep friendship, almost familial, rooted certainly in their history of intimacy but transmuted into something different.

It had happened to others within their circle of friends. They'd first met Lois when Peg started going out with her. Lois was a dance instructor, and perhaps they'd all fallen a little in love with the dark hair she piled atop her head, her dark eyes and fluid gestures. Like all of Peg's affairs, it lasted, only a few months but Lois had remained part of the group, bonded to them.

Evelyn had lived with Irene for seven years; Irene had helped her raise her children, two boys who were a handful. They'd fought almost the whole time, and Carolyn could remember nights Irene had spent drinking beer with Fran in their kitchen, unable to go home because Evelyn had thrown her out. Irene and Evelyn's breakup had been no less dramatic, full of accusation and blame, but somehow Evelyn too had been retained, held within the circle. Others came and went, passions cooling not into friendship but bitter animosity or worse, indifference.

Only she and Fran had lasted, all these years.

For all her drive and glamour, Peg had had nothing steady, nothing that lasted beyond six or nine months, a year at most. For the past decade she'd been drawn to a parade of ever-younger women, women who wanted to go dancing at late-night clubs, women with tattoos, women who found nothing more tiresome than talking with a group of women nearly old enough to be their grandmothers. Jean haunted a series of self-help groups, with names like "True Love After Fifty" and "Overcoming Fears of Intimacy," but still managed to disapprove of everyone to whom she was introduced.

Fifteen years ago, Lois had fallen in love with a woman who lived in Mexico; since neither would give up her homeland for the other, they saw each other once or twice a year, exchanged increasingly infrequent letters and phone calls. After Irene, Evelyn claimed to have given up, insisting that she was most contented when she was alone, making an art of solitude, yet in private she was always asking, "Isn't there someone you could introduce me to?" Irene was currently courting a widow from the softball team, who seemed definitely flattered but who, Irene's friends had decided, hadn't a clue about the nature of Irene's overtures.

Over the years, their friends had marveled at the couple's longevity. They'd been frequently asked – by a friend in the throes of heartbreak or by her stricken ex – to what they owed their constancy. These desperate women were looking for a formula, some magic, and they always seemed a little let down by Fran's terse reply, "It's hard work."

For Carolyn, it never seemed like work, or at least, not the onerous kind. It was work like raking leaves on a bright October morning, when the sky is a crisp blue and the sun warms your back but not too much, and you feel thankful for the task. It was work like slicing apples for a pie, stealing a tart wedge to munch on and the smell of cinnamon flooding your mouth. She never knew what to say to the red-eyed women that pressed for her secret. They always seemed to be wanting something different than whatever they had, while she had never wanted anything but Fran.

A swell of tears now threatened to overwhelm her. To escape it, Carolyn hoisted her body from the hold of the couch and made her way outside to the garage Fran had used as a tool shed. She pushed open the door, spilling warmth and daylight into the dark, cool space. A swarm of scents engulfed her – sawdust and solvents, dried leaves and gasoline. Fran had not been able to come out here the last couple of months, and a fine layer of dust covered the woodworking benches, but the rows of tools still hung in orderly progression, everything in top repair. Fran had once told her, "I'm happiest when I know I've made something with my own hands," and Carolyn had envied the wood, transformed beneath Fran's careful, determined fingers. Carolyn ran her palm lightly over the ragged teeth of a saw blade. How could Irene and Peg and the rest really think she would want to give these things away?

Carolyn sat in the middle of the cement floor, feeling its cool dampness seep into her hips and legs. Tonight they would ache, she knew, with no one there to rub them until she fell asleep, but for the moment she didn't care. Surrounded by planks of planed wood, she had a feeling like she used to get in church when she was a little girl, a sense of wonder and vastness. As when she'd been a child, awe made her turn her face in the direction of the sky. She stared up into the rough grain of the wood ceiling, eyes tracing the patterns she found.

It was then she noticed a brown cardboard carton poised on the rafters, and without even needing to investigate, she suddenly remembered what it was. As if it were yesterday, Carolyn recalled the morning years ago when Peg had zoomed into their driveway, this box poking out the top of her little red MG. "I can't have this stuff in my house anymore," Peg had insisted, referring to the contents of the carton, things that Lois had left behind when their relationship ended. This was in the first few weeks of their separation, when activities had to be planned with care so as not to include both women. Fran had patiently agreed to take the carton off Peg's hands, intending to give the items over to a rummage sale, but she must have forgotten all about it.

Carolyn rose from the floor to drag the wooden stepladder into the center of the room. She opened it up, making sure to place the stops in a locked position. Slowly, she climbed, coming to precarious balance on the top step to reach the carton. "Easy does it, now," she heard Fran say, and it steadied her.

The carton was coated with dust and left a trail of grime across her sweater as she hugged it to her chest to carry it down. Thorough, wanting to leave this room as Fran had left it, she returned the ladder to its place against the wall before resettling herself on the cement floor and turning her attention to the box.

On the lid, still visible through the accumulated layers of soot, the word "LOIS" was slashed in Peg's impatient hand. Carolyn slit the tape that held the lid in place and opened it. Despite the tape, a few generations of spiders had nested in the top of the carton, leaving behind the woolly circles of abandoned egg sacs, but the contents seemed undisturbed. The items inside were commonplace: some novels, a few vinyl record albums, an old pair of suede boots, a silk shirt the shade of periwinkle – Lois's favorite color – and a still-new-looking, porcelain-faced doll that Carolyn suspected had been a gift to Lois from Peg. For Carolyn, they were simply objects, yet for Peg they'd held the power to keep her locked in the past.

The women in their circle had always helped each other this way, moving one's possessions to a new home after a traumatic break-up, pitching in to paint rooms or lay new carpet in the effort to blot out memory. They'd grown accustomed to starting over, trying again, believing that just around the corner would be perfect love, enduring companionship. It was the same for them at sixty as it had been at thirty: With the demise of each relationship, they cleaned out their closets, sweeping away the evidence of failure, of dashed hope, and resolved to start over, to get on with their lives.

Though not unkind, she and Fran had always felt a little smug, observing the repeated drama in the lives of their friends. Perhaps the two of them had even quietly mocked these efforts to begin anew, the eternal optimism, but on this morning it seemed to Carolyn that these women had an awesome bravery. She could not help marveling at it, this skill they'd used to survive the disappointments of the years, this secret they were trying to share with her now.

And understanding this, she could finally be grateful, humbled in fact by their generosity. They, of course, had lost Fran too, but they marshaled themselves to come to Carolyn's aid with all the knowledge they possessed.

Still she knew she did not share their courage. She was not like the widows on Irene's softball team, seeking out new hobbies, keeping busy; not like her friends, embracing the future, picking up the pieces to try to fashion a new life. Her life had been with Fran and she resolved to not give up one more bit of it without a fight.

She gathered herself up off the floor once more, clutching the box, feeling the creak of her bones as she stood, giving the work bench a last loving stroke with her hand before she left the garage. Her friends would be disappointed in her, she knew, but they would come to accept it, even if they never understood. That was how they were with one another.

the arc of plot

A story is not the same as life, I warn my writing students. Life, I insist, is plotless. Random. One thing happens, then another. Always another.

My students look at me blankly, or slide their eyes down to the mottled table top, or shift their gaze to the yellow walls, which appear a little sickly under the fluorescent lights. The low whisper of the air conditioning fills the silence of the classroom. It's an unseasonably hot night for December, even in Los Angeles. Santa Ana winds have sent the temperatures into the low nineties all this week, igniting brush fires in the canyons and road rage on the crowded freeways. The winds sweep away the customary blanket of ochre smog, but leave us restless and dissatisfied. They animate the inner demons, intensify the shade of every mood. Melancholy deepens its blues; fury sparks in violent red; the gray of ennui threatens to swallow everything in sight.

Thirty minutes ago I was sitting in the parking lot with snot and tears streaming down my face, sobs shuddering in my chest. As gusts buffeted my little Honda, I wanted nothing so much as to turn the key in the ignition and drive away. I couldn't imagine how I would pull it together to face my class, put on the persona of calm authority, a loving coach for their creativity, and stand before them for two hours in that guise. But I am faithful to my obligations, so here I am, nose blown, my makeup restored.

We tell stories, I instruct the group, to confer meaning. To give form to the shapelessness of life.

I want them to appreciate the contrivance of plot – beginning, middle, end. I'm tired of stories that are too much like life: something happens, then it stops; we don't know why.

I stand at the head of the long table around which thirteen students slump in folding chairs. Five men, eight women, mostly in their thirties. Some are drawn to this free weekly workshop at the Gay and Lesbian Center because they want to capture their lives on paper, but others come, week after week, because they need a reason to leave their charmless single apartments, their microwaved dinners in front of the TV, to have someplace to go on a Wednesday night.

When I first began teaching, twenty years ago, I thought that working with adult students would mean that everyone would be motivated, disciplined, more like colleagues than students. What I've learned is that the habits of the grade school classroom are deeply ingrained; the challenge of learning still provokes anxiety, the suggestion of homework always elicits a groan. And the teacher is a figure of authority, to be worshipped or resisted, placated or undermined.

Rita has her head down on the desk, as if she's in kindergarten and it's nap time. Her face is turned away from me. Kevin has a magazine in his lap; my words compete for his attention with airbrushed bodies of nude musclemen. Ondine plays with the run that has laddered her lime green tights, poking one finger through the hole in the threads, making it widen and spread.

A story is a record of change, I inform them. We tell stories in order to make sense of change.

Luis is bright and truculent. He scratches one big ear with the tip of his pen. I can see him puzzling over this concept, trying to think of a story in which no change occurs so that he can prove me wrong.

If there is no change, I continue, you may have a great prose piece, but you haven't really got a story.

Luis retracts the point of his pen and scowls, stymied. He sits up straighter in his chair, folds his AIDS-thin arms across his chest, resting his hands in his armpits.

Plot is the device we use to give shape to a story.

I pluck up a dry erase marker and step to the white board to draw the shape of an arc with a long sweep of my arm. I label it, "The Arc of Plot."

In life, I tell them, shape is murky. How do we really know when something begins, or when it's truly over? I trace again the curved line on the white board. The arc of plot is the structure by which the change – and therefore the meaning – within a story is revealed.

In blue marker, I draw a stick figure at the left-hand base of the arc. It's the protagonist who undergoes the change. By taking action and confronting obstacles – I make little X's along the curve of the arc – the protagonist arrives at the end of the story different than how she or he began. The stick figure I draw at the right-hand base is green, not blue.

Ondine raises a languid hand, tipped with long acrylic nails painted a frosty celadon. They glow against her deep brown skin. "Could you give us an example?" she asks, "What kind of change are you talking about?"

I sigh inwardly. My students want everything pre-packaged, user-friendly. I sometimes wonder how they can manage to write when they seem so reluctant to think. I'm not usually impatient with them; maybe it's the wind that has me on edge. Mostly I sigh because I'm unprepared to respond.

"Uh, su-ure," I draw out the word, stalling. I furrow my forehead as if I am sifting through too many possibilities, considering and discarding. In fact, my brain is suddenly reduced to a state of pre-literacy; I cannot remember the plot of a single story, novel, movie or play. I am blank as a newborn. Every eye in the room is focused on me as I try to conceal this fact.

"I know," I muster a false heartiness. "Let's make something up." This is always dangerous since I'm never quite sure what might pop out of my subconscious, or theirs, but in this moment I can think of no other option.

I take a brown marker and bisect the arc with two vertical lines, so that it is divided into three segments. At the top of the board I write, "Beginning," "Middle," " End" in the corresponding sections of the curve.

"So, who can tell me the six elements that belong in the beginning of a story?" The group looks at me with dull expressions, as if to deflect my question. They're not stupid, just loathe to be called on in class. "Rita?" I prod.

She does not sit up, but instead props her chin on cupped hands and asks, "Uh… a protagonist?"

"Bingo." Then, to the whole group, "So, help me out here – who is our protagonist?"

"She should be a writing teacher," Ginger shoots back with a smile full of mischief. She's got a gold ring in her pierced eyebrow, a silver stud in her tongue that I can sometimes glimpse when she speaks. I've wanted to ask her what it's like to kiss with that, but I wouldn't want her to get the wrong idea.

"Dark hair. Cool glasses. Early forties, but she dresses hip," Luis contributes from the other side of the table.

Should I be flattered? I suppose I asked for it. I want to pull the plug, steer this session in another direction, but it's too late. The best tactic is to appear unrattled.

"Okay," I agree, keeping my voice neutral, "our protagonist is a writing teacher in her early forties. What else do we need to set up the story?"

"We need to establish the setting," Kevin has closed the magazine. Everyone in the room, in fact, is more attentive, sensing the possibility for things to veer out of control.

"It's L.A., man, 1998," Ondine informs him. "City of Angels. City of cell phones. City of selling oranges at intersections to men on cell phones in shiny BMW's." She's a decent poet when she applies herself.

"Okay," I attempt to recap. "We've got our protagonist..."

"What's her name?" Henry wants to know. Still in his twenties, he's a beautiful Vietnamese boy, though his skin is pitted with acne. His stories are transparent autobiography, in which a young Asian man is always the tragic victim. No amount of gentle critique can persuade him from this stance.

"Her name is Terry!" Luis insists.

My students look at me, wonder how far I'll let this go. I wonder myself. "So our protagonist is Terry," I repeat, "and our setting is end-of-the-millennium Los Angeles. What other elements need to be in place?"

"What's her conflict?" This from Ginger. I gaze around the room, wait to see who will supply her with a dilemma to resolve.

If everything's fine, I've told them in the past, there's no need for story, because there's no need for change.

No one speaks; they're waiting for me. The moment stretches too long, frays. What's her conflict, I think to myself, trying to force my brain to turn away from its only thought, the one it's speeding toward like a bullet train. The careful little wall I keep between myself as teacher and the rest of my life begins to crumble, a few loose bricks breaking into bits at my feet.

"Let's say… I don't know… what if she's…uh…in love with someone who can't love her back," I propose, trying my best to appear as if this idea has just popped unbidden out of my imagination. They don't know much of anything about my life, I reason.

"Can't love her back, or just doesn't love her back?" Rita queries. There's a bitterness in her voice to which I resonate. Her stories are always dark, caustic, and she's merciless on herself during critiques.

"Can't, I think," is what I answer. "There's more conflict that way, more dramatic possibility."

"So what's the name of this person you're in love with?" It's the first time tonight that Richard's spoken up. He's a quiet, serious man who writes odd, despairing little fables of modern life that are inexplicably affecting.

"You mean, that *she's* in love with?" I correct him. I always insist that we talk about characters in the third person, no matter how much the writer declares them autobiographical. When we write about ourselves, I've told them, we're always creating fiction.

"Remember," I chuckle, "this is fiction." To my own ears this protest rings hollow. So I continue. "Let's call her Vivienne."

I invent for her a name that disguises her identity, her ethnicity. Even fictionally concealed, her image springs before my eyes, her shining dark curls, the Aztec planes of her face, her full lips. It shakes me. Even all these months later, I'm stunned at the ferocity with which hurt rakes my sternum like a clawed hand. My knees sway with momentary vertigo. All of a sudden I feel ripped open, here in front of my class. Can they tell?

"So, would she be considered the antagonist?" Rita is sitting up now, sipping from her Starbuck's cup.

"Not in the beginning." A few more bricks clatter around me, raise a little red dust. For a moment I can't tell if I've spoken or only thought the words, but the students nod, appear satisfied. I feel as if any moment I might plunge into quicksand and sink from sight, but the teacher in me is brisk and efficient, keeps moving ahead with the lesson. "What other elements do we need?"

Kitt raises her hand. "The catalyst," she volunteers. "What sets the story in motion?"

I nod, add this to the white board. When I answer, I attempt to sound as if I'm crafting the story, inventing as I go. I have no way to know if anyone is fooled by this, but it allows me to continue.

"What if…before this heartbreak there was another?" I suggest. "Let's suppose that before this story begins, Terry was in a long-term relationship, like a lesbian marriage."

I'm relieved that no one in this class has been a student of mine for long. That's the beauty of a beginning class; it renews itself each year, like skin.

Ginger wags her hand at me. "How long?" she wants to know.

"Three years?" Kevin suggests with a gulp, as if that period were only slightly less than eternity.

"No," Rita snaps, "Longer than that. Like ten years or something."

"Shit!" This strains Kevin's considerable imagination.

"Of course, there were some problems," I continue, "Just like in any relationship. But there was a bond, a commitment."

"Then one day her partner announces that she's in love with some secretary at work," Luis cuts in, "and–bam–the lesbian marriage is history." His mouth curls in a twisted smile, as if he takes perverse pleasure in the disaster he's just wreaked.

I could quibble about the details, but he's pretty much nailed it. It wasn't all that long ago–a year, a year and a half. I can remember days when I came in to teach, sleepless and shell-shocked. I would stand before my classes scarcely able to construct a persona with which to interact with them. I disclosed more than I should have, unable to contain my grief, driven to seek comfort from any quarter. Those students were sympathetic and solicitous; they left me encouraging messages on my phone machine, shyly handed me greeting cards with inspirational messages and scrawled inducements to "hang in there." One sent me to her psychic; another brought flowers.

Some of the women students, the ones with whom I'd grown particularly close, came on moving day, carried my meager belongings–unmatched furniture, boxes of books, armloads of clothing, garbage bags stuffed with underwear–from my home where tall windows looked out onto lemon trees to the squat stucco house I had hastily rented. I gave myself over to their care, upending the roles of teacher and student. They made up my shabby bed, loaned me appliances, filled the house with lighted candles and smudged the rooms with sticks of burning sage.

I am so grateful that none of them is in this class now. The students who sit before me have never witnessed the dust balls under my desk, nor seen me collapse on the kitchen linoleum to weep.

"So, the catalyst is the first loss," I pull myself out of my reverie and once more address the class. "Our protagonist is hurt, she's vulnerable. Everything she once thought was solid has dissolved."

"Does that help to establish the stakes?" Richard wants to know.

"Absolutely," I quickly add "Stakes" to the white board.

"That's when Vivienne appears," Ondine declares, eager for the story to begin.

And she was like a miracle, calm as the earth, a stable foundation, crooning, "You can rest here. I'll be safe for you." A voice on the other end of the phone – "Call anytime," she offered – first thing in the morning as she got ready for work, or keeping me company late at night as I ate steamed shrimp and vegetables from the takeout Chinese deli. On moving day she took me to Ikea to buy a dresser so my underwear wouldn't have to stay in garbage bags; she navigated me through the crowded aisles, her hand on the small of my back. And how I leaned into that warm pressure, let it guide and steady me.

"How do they meet?" Kitt wonders. She's a pudgy woman with a child's face and a head full of blonde dreadlocks. She's always talking about what she wants to write, but I have yet to see her complete anything.

Ginger's got an idea about that. "I think Terry's known her for a long time," she proposes. "Vivienne's had her eye on Terry for years, and now she sees her chance."

I nod, as if this is only one more detail, a small complexity of plot. "That could heighten the stakes, because there's already a connection with Vivienne that Terry would want to preserve."

"And because they know each other," Rita interjects, "Terry lets her guard down more quickly than she would with a stranger."

What I won't tell them is that she was my student. For six years. One of my favorites – big talent, an original voice, a lot of attitude in the classroom. It would freak them out, and rightly so. I always insisted I would never get involved with a student, although I used to imagine it was a matter of their protection, rather than my own.

"So how do they get together?" Ginger is eager to know.

"They do a few things – go to the movies, have dinner, go to a reading, a play," I suggest. "Then Terry invites Vivienne to be her escort at a community fundraiser, a formal dance."

"Whoa, dress-up!" Henry preens, and his face grows dreamy, conjuring a vision of the scene. "Vivienne's in a black suit; she's stylin'. Terry's in a long black dress, like from the forties, all big shoulders and narrow waist."

I remember that night so vividly. Miles Davis' *Kinds of Blue* on my stereo as she came to pick me up. She brought me a corsage, white roses, and I was touched as she pinned it in my hair.

"And they dance together real close and steamy," Luis taunts.

"Cheek to cheek!" Ondine teases. "Is this the night when they do it?"

"Not yet," I caution. "We need some conflict to keep the story going. They dance, there's electricity, but Terry thinks it's way too soon for her to get involved. When Vivienne takes her home, she tries to kiss Terry, but Terry says no."

"Oh, that's cold," Luis protests, then adds, "but it does prolong the dramatic suspense."

Still, it occurs to me that maybe all of this is only prologue; maybe the true catalyst for the story is the night she lost her keys. One week after she'd slow-danced with me, that night I'd sent her home unkissed, she came to hear me give a reading, as she'd done faithfully all those years she'd been my student. Sometime during the reading her house and car keys disappeared. Afterward, we made a frantic search of the bookstore, retraced her steps from parking lot to entrance, shone a flashlight through her car windows – nothing.

I offered to help – how could I not, kind as she had been to me. I was willing to wait while she called a mobile locksmith, but she was rattled, wanted to wait until morning to deal with it. I would have driven her home, helped her break in but, as she puzzled, how would she get back the next day?

That's how she ended up at my place, spending the night. Wearing my t-shirt. Wedged onto one side of my bed. Who was I kidding? Every nerve in my body alive to her nearness, the smell of her hair against my pillow. It was a hot night. An exquisite torture – my desire for her at war with my resolve not to transgress that boundary.

"So, does that introduce the central question?" Kitt inquires.

I blink at her for a moment, unable to recall the last words I'd spoken aloud. Despite the air conditioning, I am sweating, my back damp, underarms clammy, as if the hot wind blowing through the city streets had entered the building, swept its way down the halls, insinuated itself into this yellow room.

Kitt seems unaware of my hesitation. "Is it: 'Does Terry relent and get together with Vivienne?'"

"Or maybe," Ginger interjects, "the ex gets jealous and realizes she lost a good thing with Terry."

"That can't be it," Henry protests. "Don't you remember what she said about the conflict: 'The protagonist is in love with someone who can't love her back?'"

"I know!" Kevin volunteers. "Maybe Vivienne can't love her because she's from an alien culture that doesn't allow intergalactic romance." Kevin's stories are always filled with aliens and rocket ships and intergalactic sex.

"That's an interesting idea," I try not to sound dismissive, "but I think this story should be a little more realistic than that."

I scrawl "Central Question" on the board, the final element needed for the set-up. "Remember how I've told you that in the beginning of a story we can think the central question is one thing, but as events unfold that question might actually change?"

In the beginning, my resistance had many reasons: it was too soon for me; she was my student. She didn't fit the profile of my imagined partner – someone whose ambitions burned bright as my own, someone who wanted a big life too. Later, though, I would grow to cherish the differences between us: the rich garden of her inner life, the dreams that bloomed like rare, exotic flowers; her capacity for comfort, the ability to find pleasure in everyday life, soothing as spiced milk. These qualities were a soft bed of fertile earth in which I could plant myself, in which I might grow.

I worried that I had too much power: I was older, her teacher. She confessed she'd had a crush on me the whole time she'd been in my classes. She showed me poems she'd written in that state of longing. She had snapshots of me on her refrigerator, her desk at work. I was moved, humbled; she'd carried these feelings for six years, coals kept kindled inside her heart. Could I ever care for her the same way? The first night we kissed she looked at me with eyes like dark lakes and said, "Don't hurt me."

"Initially," I answer my students, "we do wonder if they'll ever get together. Vivienne pursues her, but Terry has misgivings. Even after she succumbs, she still holds part of herself in reserve."

"So first we wonder if they're gonna do it, then we wonder if Terry is gonna be a bitch to Vivienne," Luis synopsizes.

Luis is pushing his luck; he knows I'll let him get away with it. To bust him for his insolence would only serve to narrow the gap between myself and the fictional "Terry."

I ignore him. "All right," I challenge the group, "what happens next?"

"Despite herself, girlfriend's gonna fall in love with Vivienne," Ondine smiles, catching the tip of her tongue between her wide teeth, savoring this turn of events.

"Would that be a reversal?" Richard asks.

I've taught them that a story cannot proceed too smoothly toward its conclusion. A protagonist may appear to be headed in one direction, then turn around and do the opposite. Like that first night I kissed her, falling into the sweet abyss of her mouth. I kept insisting, "I can't do this," right up until the moment I let her pull me into her arms.

"The more she fights it, the harder she falls," Ondine's eyes spark.

How hard I fell. My heart cracked open without thought for the consequences, as if lightning would never strike twice in the same place. The last years of my "marriage" I'd felt so neglected, unconsidered; now here was someone who seemed to notice everything I did and felt and needed. She remembered a pink sweater I'd worn once to class years earlier. She pestered me to lock my car door, fearful that someone might break in and hijack me. She paid a coworker to crochet me an afghan, so I wouldn't be cold the nights I didn't see her. She brought me little household items—a colander, a new shower head – that she'd observed I was missing; I felt like she was looking out for me

Our second night together she ran a bath for me, lit the house with candles, brewed a cup of tea. Finally settled on her sheets, I nestled into her body, while she asked me how I wanted to be touched. Here is someone who can really love me, I told myself, and I could scarcely fathom my luck.

As I fell, I came to cherish everything about her: the curves of her hips, her stories of growing up with eight brothers and sisters, the look of relief and contentment that stole over her face when she ate something she really liked. I sent bouquets of flowers to her office, baked the cornbread with maple syrup she liked so well, soaped her hair in the shower, my fingers massaging her scalp.

A thousand times I've asked myself why I fell so deeply. I'd meant to be so careful, although at the time my only thought was for being careful with her; I thought I held all the cards. Once I stepped off the ledge, though, I began to plummet, no longer in control of how far or how fast the drop. In my marriage, I'd always held certain boundaries, habits or stances I refused to alter, ferocious about being true to myself. Perhaps I was determined not to make the same mistake; perhaps I was so shattered by that ending that I had no more boundaries to defend. Not only was I willing, I longed to let her change me.

"But," Rita interjects, pulling me back from my musing, "the minute Terry falls in love with her, Vivienne starts to pull back." Rita scowls at her fingernails, hands splayed on the table top. "That's a reversal."

I almost gasp. Could these students know more about me than I'd realized? Did they gossip about me when they went for coffee after class? Or is this a predictable twist, predictable to everyone but me?

"Oooh," Ondine winces, "That ain't right."

"Vivienne stops returning phone calls," Kevin expounds, "says she wants to date other people."

Ginger takes it a step further, "Terry runs into her coming out of the movies one night with a gorgeous blonde!"

It wasn't quite that bad. Still, nothing in the beginning of our relationship could have prepared me for her reversal. She, who had courted me so hard, began to retreat. She would no longer talk on the phone at night, insisting it disturbed her sleep. She would no longer see me during the week, and usually only one night on the weekends. Although she still swore she loved me, she began to say that it would never work out between us, that we should pull the plug. "I can break your heart now, or I can break it later," she said to me.

I grapple for an explanation. "Vivienne begins to be afraid. She finally gets something she wanted for a long time, and it terrifies her. She can't tolerate it. She flees."

"So, this is where the 'love interest' character becomes the antagonist?" Richard wonders.

"I suppose it is," my words betray a certain reluctance. "But remember, not every antagonist is a villain. They don't always intend to thwart or harm the protagonist. Often their actions are what make the protagonist change and grow."

Why do I defend her, make excuses? I can't bear for anyone to think ill of her.

"In her own story, Vivienne may not be a villain," Rita allows. "But in Terry's story, she sure the hell is!"

But I can't bring myself to see it that way. Maybe I try to tell myself her story to make my own less painful. In that story, she's a woman at war with herself, protagonist and antagonist in the same skin. The one who loves me, the one who cannot overcome her fear.

She tells a different version. She says, "It just didn't work out." She says, "We're too different." She says, "I just don't feel the same way about you." And what choice do I have but to believe her?

"So isn't this the point where the central question changes again?" Kevin asks.

"It sure is," Kitt answers. "Now it's all about: is Terry going to lose Vivienne?"

"And what happens to the stakes?" I query.

"They get heightened," Henry replies. "Is Terry gonna get dumped a second time? We're worried for her."

And with good reason. The answer to his question is, of course, yes, but for the longest time I wouldn't see it. I wanted to live inside her story, my version of her story, to engage in her struggle; I believed that love could win out over fear. I thought if I could just hold still for long enough, she might learn to be safe with me. I comforted myself with the fact that she always came back. But then she always went away again, further and further, taking more with her each time.

I think about one August afternoon we visited the new aquarium in Long Beach. She'd stopped sleeping with me by then, but I awakened that morning to an email from her. "I love you so much," it said, "and I'm looking forward to spending the day with you." An encouraging signal. We went to brunch beside the ocean, traded bites over a view of the sun-sparked waves. Our conversation was animated, momentarily purged of the strained moods and awkward silences that had come to punctuate our interactions.

Then we retreated from the midday glare into the cool darkness of the aquarium. We were like children, palms smudging the glass of the huge tanks – "Look at the colors on that one!" "Hey, check out this big guy." We were transported in that underwater world, however simulated. Her hand on the small of my back.

"Let's take a trip to the Sea of Cortez," I suggested. We used to always talk about where we would travel. She smiled, agreed. It was a plan for the future, our future, and I held it close. In the gift store she bought me a silver chain, a slave bracelet. She knelt there on the carpet, in front of all those families on their Sunday outings, to fasten it around my bare ankle. She told me it looked sexy.

Every moment that day spoke to our intimacy. Our dinner of fish tacos at a place we'd always liked to go, our stroll through the health food store, a remembered familiarity of shopping together. Back at her house, the evening waning, she encouraged me to stay a while, lie with her on her narrow couch. Her arms around me, my head on her shoulder. When I tilted my face up for a kiss, she pulled away. "I am not your lover," she insisted, "I can't do this with you."

"Then what is it you've been doing all day?" I demanded, tearful, incredulous. It all erupted then, each moment of that day detonating, leaving us both charred, ashes on our tongues. Some gate inside her clanged shut and I was left on the other side, howling to be let back in.

"This is a story with a long middle," I tell my students. "Sometimes Vivienne is right there, acting like a lover. But whenever they start to get close, Vivienne backs away again."

Kitt shakes her pale dreadlocks in sympathy. "Intermittent reinforcement," she frowns. "And Terry's stuck on that roller coaster. When Vivienne's in the picture, Terry's happy. When they're on the outs, she's miserable."

"She doesn't sleep. She gets real skinny. She cries every day," Ondine orchestrates each point with a sweep of her long fingers; her green nails flash across my field of vision.

Henry adds, "Yeah, and her friends get sick of her. It keeps going back and forth."

"But that makes it suspenseful," Richard argues. "There are all these twists and turns. We don't really know how it's going to turn out."

"It's not suspenseful," Rita growls. "It's goddamned predictable. There's only one way it can turn out."

"So why doesn't Terry just dump her?" Ondine wants to know.

"Maybe she really loves her," I suggest. "Maybe she believes that underneath it all, Vivienne loves her."

"That's not love," Luis insists.

"Maybe she can't dump Vivienne." There's an edge of hysteria to Rita's voice. "Maybe she's hooked. She keeps thinking if she just hangs in, she can win." Her eyes are beginning to tear. She swipes at them, a furious gesture, leaving trails of smudged eyeliner like bruises at each temple.

I have a sudden flash of understanding: she hasn't been reading my secret diaries, or eavesdropping on my therapy sessions. Rita's gone through something like this herself. Maybe she's still going through it.

"The best thing she could do is walk away," Ginger advises, like a "Dear Abby" with piercings. "That's what's gonna make Vivienne want her again."

How many times have I heard these same arguments from my friends? How many times did I collapse on their couches, across tables in uncountable restaurants, flooding out the latest episode of a saga that seemed like it would never end?

"The central question is changing again," Henry points out. "Now it's: 'How is Terry going to get free?'"

Ginger disagrees. "I think it's: 'how much can a girl take?'"

"Or," Richard suggests, "'how does she survive this new loss?'"

"How many times can the question change in a story?" Kitt wants to know. Her round face bears a worried expression. "Won't the reader get frustrated at some point?"

Frustrated, yes. Sick to death of it, I think, but the teacher answers smoothly, "Not as long as each question proceeds from the one before with a kind of inevitability."

"Okay," Luis challenges, "but how does the protagonist change? That's what you're supposed to be telling us." His black eyes bore straight into mine.

"Yeah," Ginger concurs, "I'm ready to smack her for being such a victim."

I've told my students that between the middle and the end of a story, the protagonist must undergo a "Decisive Moment." We cannot sympathize with a protagonist who is solely the victim of outside events. The decisive moment is one in which the protagonist becomes the agent of her own change.

So what is my decisive moment? It is exactly this question I've wrestled with for so long. I've done acupuncture, bodywork, yoga, and homeopathy. I've seen a psychic, read tarot cards, thrown the I Ching, consulted my astrological chart, burned candles at the full moon. I've cried every day for six months; I've spent thousands of dollars on therapy. I've unearthed the little girl in the lavender jumper, alone and waiting late into the night for her parents to come home from the bar. I've revisited the rebellious teenager, clutching a bottle of Cuervo and a smoldering joint. I've crooned to the woman abandoned by her lover of nine years. Still, the resolution of this story remains as elusive as the first time she said, "I don't want to see you anymore."

"How do you think she changes?" I throw it back to the group. Feel free to play god, I want to tell them. See if you can make Terry do or feel what I haven't been able to.

"Girlfriend gets fed up with bouncin' on the end of someone else's yo-yo," Ondine wags one celadon-tipped finger. "She jumps that tired string."

"Yeah, she gets some self-respect, stands up for her herself," Ginger echoes, her voice rising as if delivering an anthem.

Richard is thoughtful. "I think Vivienne finally pushes her too far. Maybe she goes back and forth one too many times, or maybe she does something especially awful, but it's the last straw."

"I know!" Henry exclaims, a bit too eagerly, "Maybe they have this major fight, and Terry punches her lights out."

Kevin breaks in, "Or else Terry's abducted by aliens, and she gets this really galactic view of the situation, and realizes that Vivienne's not the one for her anyway."

The group is electrified by their solutions to the protagonist's dilemma. It's part wish fulfillment, I'm sure, things they've fantasized doing but haven't, couldn't. That's some of what fiction does for us; we can portray ourselves as stronger, braver versions than we are in our ordinary flawed lives.

"Maybe she takes everything Vivienne ever gave her and makes a big bonfire!" Henry's eyes light up.

"No, no," Kitt objects. "She just says, 'Leave me the fuck alone, don't call, drop dead, have a nice life.'" She raises one arm in the air, snaps her fingers for punctuation.

"Then she gets a new haircut, drops ten pounds, and looks so fabulous that Vivienne eats her heart out," Ginger adds.

"And then, she meets someone terrific who falls madly in love with her," Kitt concludes, "and they live happily ever after."

"Wait a minute," I interrupt them. "Is that story believable?"

Luis shakes his head, but everyone else is saying, "Sure," "Hell, yeah," "Why not?" until Rita breaks in.

"What if she just can't change?" Rita asks, with such quiet intensity that everyone in the room quiets down. Her harsh tone has dissolved into a plea. Shoulders hunched, a flush burns on each cheek. She's gripping her spiral notebook so hard her knuckles have gone pale beneath her dusky skin. "I mean, I know she needs to for the story and all, but what if she can't?"

Her despair calls out to mine with the lure of children's voices on a summer afternoon. My misery wants to push open the screen door, snatching up a quarter for the ice cream truck, run out into the full light of day to join the others. Instead, like a child deformed and hideous, the secret shame of the household, it must stay confined to the dark and airless attic of my skin. It has no place in this classroom, yowling and spitting and drooling, making everyone embarrassed or afraid.

A story is not the same as life. My students want to craft an ending that ensures that not only will Terry be all right, she will triumph. She's come through a harrowing loss, but she's learned from it, grown stronger, is determined to love again. How can I blame them? It's what every reader wants from a story.

But in life, our protagonist goes on for a long time in that state of stunned grief, sleepwalking through errands to the grocery store, crosstown freeway commutes, her first trip to France, the workshops in which she assumes the persona of teacher, pretending to be someone with wisdom to offer. It is possible that she may never understand why this happened, or what she was meant to learn. Maybe she will spin forever in Vivienne's orbit, an unclaimed moon in weak gravity.

"If she can't change," I answer Rita softly, "then maybe the story just isn't over yet."

And perhaps mine isn't either. My decision would never satisfy my students. I haven't stormed out, told her off, sought revenge, or thrown myself into someone else's arms; I haven't severed the bond. We still talk on the phone, go to dinner, the occasional movie, buy each other spontaneous gifts – a book, a shirt, a CD. In her story we are learning to be friends. In mine, I simply continue to love her, without hope of reciprocity. Sometimes this is almost enough; the rest of the time I tell myself that I am learning something about keeping my heart open. Sometimes hope still surfaces, like a blossom in a hostile season, all the more poignant for its evident impossibility.

This is what I hate about life, its messiness and ambiguity. Did my story begin with my break-up, with the first night I danced with "Vivienne," or was it the first moment she walked into a class six years ago? And did it conclude when she said, "No more; I want to move on?" or is it still to end in some future we have not yet lived and cannot even imagine?

"It's nine o'clock," Richard's quiet voice nudges me.

My eyes stray to the calm face of the clock on the yellow wall; its hands dictate our beginnings and endings here.

"We have to stop," I say apologetically. "Great work, everybody; I'm impressed. You're really starting to get this arc of plot thing. See you next Wednesday."

My students stand and file out, letting in the heat from the hallway as they prop open the door. Rita is the first to go, out of the door like a shot, and I resist the urge to call after her. Kevin ambushes me with a question about the due date for another assignment – is it flexible?

It is Luis who lingers when everyone else is gone. "Are you all right?" he asks, and his voice is tender. And I realize that he understands the way that story and life can blur and blend together until boundaries dissolve. If I let him, he would wrap his bony arms around me, hug me to his too-thin frame. I could talk or not talk, cry or not cry. I see all of this offered in his black eyes.

What I've learned, though, one thing that Vivienne has taught me is that we cannot escape our roles in this drama. That no matter how astute my students, however deep the regard in which they hold me, I can be no more than a character in their lives, the beloved teacher, a fiction. I must always stand apart from them, never threaten to become too real. This is what they need from me. What she needs.

I look for a long time into Luis' eyes.. "I'm fine," I tell him quietly, and he nods, once and then again.

"Take it easy," he says as he turns.

"You too," I call out, as the door closes behind him.

I gather my notebook, my file folders. I shut down the air conditioning, feel how quickly the heat takes the room in its thick embrace. All the energy I summoned to teach, the adrenaline of performance, drains from me now, leaving my body limp and numb.

For a moment I let myself collapse into one of the metal chairs. I expect my earlier tears to return, but they don't; there is only a hollow ache in my chest and the sound of wind against the roof.

Wearily, I hoist myself up, erase the white board, the arc of plot dissolving into fine particles of color that stick to my palms. I whisper her name, her real name, but no one hears.

evalina's prayer

Even now, all these years later, I can remember the smell of the room where Evalina took me to pray. My nostrils recall the heavy scent of mildew, a damp and unused odor, barely camouflaged by the pungent overlay of incense blanketing the air. The room smelled the way it looked, old and dark and crowded, lined with shelves of crumbling books. A worn Oriental rug thinned beneath our feet, its pattern broken by large, thread-bare patches, its once-vibrant colors faded. The windows were obliterated by folds of dusty drapery; neither sunlight nor fresh air had entered that room for many years.

At the time I did not question it, but thinking back I am surprised that she would pick this space in which to offer her devotions. Maybe that's because I am not a religious person. If I were to pray, I think I'd want to do it in the sunshine, outside in a field of flowers, colors exploding all around me, someplace where I could witness the bounty of the Spirit while I thundered my petitions to the sky. Or so I imagine. As I say, I am not a religious person. If I were, perhaps I would understand what it was about that dark, neglected room that made Evalina Grimes swoon with the glory of God, a glory so profound she longed to share it with me, a gift so precious as to tempt the most ungrateful recipient.

Evalina and I had been in the same high school class, but we were not friends. In high school, Evalina was so shy that she could not speak to another human being without blushing to the roots of her thin, pale hair. She would stammer and twitch when called on by a teacher; conversations with her peers were out of the question. There was about her something rabbity – nervous, timid, her nose quivering. By some uncharacteristic mercy she wasn't picked on or tormented by the other students; Evalina was simply ignored. She seemed, as far as anyone could tell, fully grateful for the inattention.

I, on the other hand, spent my high school years worrying about my breasts, which were larger than those of any other girl in school. This fact provided me with loads of attention, much of it unwanted, as in the dumbfounded stares of acne'd boys, catty rumors spread by envious girls and unabashed leers of certain male instructors. I couldn't tell whether I felt more blessed or cursed with this endowment; the pillows of flesh seemed to have sprouted from my chest like mushrooms in the dark, alien beings that had colonized my body and which now defined me. Ambivalent as I was, I cultivated my celebrity with tight sweaters and low-cut blouses. My shape provided me with an identity, a secure set of expectations in my human interactions, and despite the drawbacks, I embraced it.

I'm not sure Evalina and I had ever spoken until we ended up at the same college. Most of our classmates had gone on to state university; only she and I found ourselves matriculated to the small, private Harrison College for Women. She was here because her mother had graduated from this same school, I because four years of concentration on the implications of my breast size had adversely affected my grade point average.

Harrison College was situated on the grounds of what had once been a lavish estate. Evalina and I were both assigned to the same dormitory, a decaying four-story building, the old Langley mansion. Brooding oil portraits of the original dwellers hung in the stairwell; their faces glowered as if disgusted by our presence in their home. The first floor boasted a massive public room, dining room and kitchen, but upstairs the rooms tended to be small and oddly shaped, utterly deficient in closet space. At eighteen, I could muster no enthusiasm for the ornate architecture of Langley Hall, which I judged decrepit and depressing; I longed for the newness and predictability of the squat, cement high-rise dorms in which my former classmates lived at State.

Upon arrival, I was assigned a roommate, Astrid, who turned out to be bulimic (we didn't have that word for it then; I just called her "weird.") Every night she would stay up methodically eating the candy bars that lined the drawers of her bureau and desk – Mars bars were her favorite, and Three Musketeers – only to regurgitate them vociferously sometime in the hours before dawn. I'd lie awake and listen to her gag and spit into a small metal wastebasket lined with a plastic bag; I suppose she did it that way to escape the unexpected scrutiny of someone who might have wandered into the communal bathroom. Either my scrutiny did not count, or she assumed – incorrectly – that I was a heavy sleeper.

I did not speak to Evalina until the third week of school. I had of course noticed her by then – our dorm housed fewer than a hundred students – but, having been in the habit of ignoring her the past four years, I had simply continued that etiquette.

Evalina, though, seemed to have outgrown her shyness. She approached me quite directly in the dining room. Looking right into my eyes, she exclaimed, "I'm so relieved to see a familiar face," without a hint of pinkness in her cheeks.

I murmured something non-committal, not certain that I shared her relief, but she was undeterred. Her gray eyes seemed to deepen as she studied me. "Christy, are you all right?"

It was my turn to blush. Owing to Astrid's nocturnal habits, I had pretty much abandoned both sleeping and eating. Shadows weighted my eyes in a haggard face, and I'd been losing weight. "I guess…uh… it's t-taking a while to adjust," I stammered, as though I were ashamed, as though I were somehow implicated in my roommate's secret ritual.

Evalina's roommate had left without warning after just one day at school; Evalina had returned from dinner that first night to find all trace of her removed. She confessed to finding it lonely, and wondered how I was getting along with mine. I could find no words with which to answer her but my face must have said it all, because in the next moment she clasped my hand and eagerly suggested, "Why don't you ask to transfer in with me?"

Before the end of the day it was accomplished; I was installed in a fourth floor room, larger and with a better window, a room in which the smell of stale vomit did not linger like a bad dream. I'd been rescued by Evalina Grimes, and now I felt myself to be reluctantly indebted to her.

Nothing about my life at college resembled my previous life. All the attention, both welcomed and dreaded, that had been showered on me for the past four years simply evaporated like a puddle on a hot day. The predictable exchanges, on which I had come to rely, no longer applied. At Harrison College. no one was interested in my physique;

among that group of college-aged woman, my breasts were in fact unremarkable, large but not inordinately so.

This left me without a distinguishing characteristic; I was neither pretty nor ugly, not terribly smart and with no talents to speak of. I had no reputation for being reckless with drugs, interested in politics or gifted at athletics. I was not burning to make the world a better place. I had decided to major in education, not because I had a calling to teach, but precisely because as a field it did not seem to require a strong preference for anything.

As the role to which I'd become accustomed disappeared like chalk outlines on a well-traveled sidewalk, I began to feel increasingly shapeless, undefined. I did not seem to know who to be nor how to interact with the vibrant, solid women who surrounded me. For the first time in my life, I found it hard to make friends. Except for Evalina.

Evalina befriended me with a ferocity I found unsettling. She worried about what I ate and encouraged me to study. She was constantly bringing home tidbits of information about groups that were forming on campus, free lectures by visiting scholars, art exhibits and dance performances – trying to entice my interest. She gave me pep talks with such cloying cheer that they lay in my gut like Astrid's nightly ratio of candy bars. Evalina was unfailingly kind to me, even when I left my clothes in rank piles on our mutual carpet, even when I lost one of the silver earrings she'd insisted that I borrow.

Life had changed for Evalina too. She'd lost that scared, rabbity quality and taken on a kind of inner glow. She conversed easily with the other women in our dorm; I was now the one who could not look them in the eye. Where Evalina threw herself into her studies with a genuine thirst for knowledge, I sat through classes numb and slack-jawed as an accident victim, scrawling notes that later I could not decipher. Evalina appeared to be well on her way to becoming herself, speeding full steam ahead, while I drifted like an unmoored vessel, trying to navigate by stars on a fog-laden night.

She was an early riser, and left our room each morning long before I'd disentangled from the blankets on my twin bed. I'd see her over breakfast, her expression bright and alert as she swilled orange juice, while the rest of us poked, bleary-eyed, at our oatmeal and tried to stoke ourselves with coffee. I always assumed that she'd been for an early-morning walk, or something equally wholesome and self-improving.

She often came in late at night as well, but I attributed this to the fact that she – a philosophy major – was a much more dedicated scholar than myself, and must have been feverishly studying until the library closed. Preoccupied as I was by my own failure to adjust to college life, my curiosity about Evalina's comings and goings was limited. I never asked.

Autumn gave way to winter, and with the dawn of each gray day I felt less connected to the life that swirled around me like the first snow blanketing the grounds of Harrison College. The barren trees, the bleak sky struck me as a cruel reflection of my own internal landscape.

Holiday break brought no relief. I spent it at my parents' house, sequestered in what was formerly my room. During my four-month absence my mother had repainted and refurnished, relegating whatever I had left behind to boxes stacked in the garage. Gone was the large stuffed tiger that Eddie Rogers had won for me two summers ago at the county fair; missing were the framed photos of me in my prom dress, the one with the plunging neck considered oh-so-daring by the chaperones, hanging on the arm of a tuxedo'd Jerry Cavanaugh. No longer pink and womblike, this room was now a cold, slate blue, with new curtains and bedspread in a matching navy; it was called "the guest room" and it no longer contained any remnant of my previous existence save for its contours.

Still, I stayed in that alien room. dodging my parents' attempts to appear interested in my life at college, my father's stern admonitions about my grades, my mother's coy inquiries about whether I was dating. I avoided, too, the few calls that filtered over the phone lines from erstwhile high school friends, inventing headaches or shouting to my mother, "I can't talk; I'm just out of the shower!" I felt like a space traveler on a botched mission, unable to return to the world from whence I had been launched, without the instruments to reach a destination.

It was my mother who wrote to Evalina, once the year had turned and we were back at Langley Hall. I can imagine my mother's earnest confession penned in her strict cursive: that she was concerned about me, that I didn't seem quite like myself; could Evalina shed any light on what was going on? I do not know what Evalina might have answered; as winter deepened, things went steadily downhill for me. I rarely bothered to go to classes anymore. I seldom dressed to go downstairs for meals. Evalina brought me crackers and a jar of peanut butter, fresh apples and cartons of milk. I mostly stayed in our room at Langley Hall. I did not read or listen to music; I could not really think of anything I wanted to do. I either lay on my unmade bed staring at the ceiling or sat before the window, watching snowflakes drift, helpless, to the ground.

If this frightened Evalina I never knew it. She continued serenely about her life, rising before the sun and returning late to our room each night. She was always gentle with me, and respectful. She never complained that it might be nice if I would bathe more frequently. She never hinted that she'd love to have the room to herself once in a while. She never once snapped and yelled, "You loser, you creep, get over it!" or suggested I return to Astrid.

What Evalina did was this. One night she came back after midnight. She stood in the doorway for a long time, staring into the gloam of the room which I had left unlit. I could feel her eyes on my back as I gazed out at the snow; neither of us spoke. Minutes passed. I could hear the rhythm of her breath, a light stirring of stale air. Then I heard her step and the soft click of the door closing as she left again.

By the time she returned I had moved from the chair to my bed where I lay, not sleeping. Without turning on the light she came over to my side and placed a cool hand on my wrist.

"Christy," she said, and her voice was calm, not urgent at all. It beckoned like a placid lake. "I want you to do something with me. Will you come?"

It's not that she was forceful, but somehow I was lifted up from the mattress, first into a sitting position, then standing beside her. There was an odd perfume about her, something I could not identify as she pulled a sweater over my ragged pajama top, and helped me to stuff my legs into jeans, my feet into moccasins. It never occurred to me to ask where we were going; I trailed Evalina and her soothing voice as if I were swimming in a dream.

She led me down the carved oak stairwell, past the disapproving glares of the dead Langleys, to the first floor. A short, narrow hallway branched off the dining room, and at the end of it, a door. It was a door I'd never paid attention to – I suppose I assumed it was a storage room or pantry – and it was locked.

Evalina slipped her plastic-coated student I.D. card from the pocket of her skirt and, in a gesture of practiced criminality that I would never have anticipated, slid the card between the door and its jam and swiftly released the bolt.

The room beyond the door must have been the old library; unlike the rest of the house it had not been restored. It was at that moment bright with the flames of two dozen candles; Evalina had prepared for my arrival. Their radiance allowed me to study the room: the wine-dark velvet curtains that muffled the windows, the shelves of books, neglected and decayed, the moth-eaten Oriental rug that spread across the floor.

From the mantle above the unlit fireplace, two cones of incense smoked in metal ashtrays confiscated from the student lounge. The smoldering cones released a heavy scent of spice into the air, the aroma I had smelled on Evalina. Beneath this masking layer of perfume lurked the odors of mildew and dust.

My long-dormant curiosity was reawakened, my brain choked with questions. I could not get one of them past my throat, could only stare at Evalina, her skin golden in the candlelight. Despite the chill of the night, she bent to remove her shoes, and indicated that I should do the same. Then she led me to the center of the room, directly underneath the dome of the ceiling. There she knelt and, at her urging, so did I.

In this environment, Evalina's face was transformed; her expression shone with an abandon and a bliss that I had only witnessed before on the features of movie stars in the midst of a love scene. She clasped one of my hands in her own and whispered, "This is where I come to pray. It helps me so much, Christy."

Her gray eyes searched the depths of mine; her look was full of hunger, the conviction that her faith would rescue me. In her gaze I saw the sea, rolling and churning, waiting to swallow me. My breath grew shallow, the weight of the ocean pressing on my chest.

"Pray with me, Christy," she implored. Her grip on my hand tightened; she held it against her heart. Her eyes slid shut then and her forehead tensed in supplication.

Everything was swirling around me, the dancing flames of the candles, the insidious plumes of scented smoke, the dreams of the all women asleep in the rooms above. Evalina's eyelids fluttered, her lips moved in soundless incantation. The roar of the ocean grew louder in my ears; it threatened to extinguish the beat of my heart. The odor of mildew and death was sinking into my bones. Whatever form I might have retained until this point was dissipating; I was dissolving into the rug, reduced to no more than dust ground into its threadbare fabric.

I know I screamed but I don't know if I made a sound. I pushed Evalina, freed myself from her grasp, sent her sprawling on the carpet. Turning as I did to flee the room, I caught one glimpse of her stricken eyes, rain falling on the sea at night.

After weeks of inactivity, I was panting by the time I reached our fourth-floor room. I shoved my feet into a pair of leather boots, hugged a winter coat around me and snatched my purse from underneath the desk. That was all I retrieved of my former life. I ran back down the stairs, no longer caring if I woke the house, and slammed the front door behind me as I escaped from Langley Hall. I trudged through drifts to the main road, where I managed to flag down a truck, heading east on a long-distance run. Only when I felt the hum of the wheels against the road, the gentle rocking of my body in head-long motion, did my breathing slow, my pulse ease.

I never did return to Harrison College. That truck took me to the city, and I stayed. I made a kind of life in that city and, over the years, in many cities. I've moved around. There've been times when I thought I knew myself and times when I lost me again, times when I got attention and times when I was content to be ignored, times when I had lots of friends and times when I kept to myself alone. Maybe I've always been adrift in that anchorless boat, trying to navigate by starlight. Sometimes the fog lifts and the night is clear, then it descends again.

When I got to that first city, on that crisp, cold morning, I found a diner and sat and drank cup after cup of coffee. I could still smell the incense in my unwashed hair, the scent of rot on my skin. I felt Evalina's cool fingers on my wrist, saw her eyelids flutter like the delicate wings of insects.

I never have found any use for religion, but over the years I've come to understand the power of Evalina's prayer. I wonder if she knows how it released me.

That morning in the city, I mailed a postcard to my parents. I thanked them for everything and told them I would be all right. To Evalina I sent nothing, not a word.

Terry Wolverton is the author of nine books: *Embers*, a novel in poems; three prose novels, *Stealing Angel, The Labrys Reunion* and *Bailey's Beads; Insurgent Muse: ife and art at the Woman's Building*, a memoir; *Breath and Other Storeis*, short fiction, and three collections of poetry: *Shadow and Praise, Mystery Bruise* and *Black Slip.*

She has also edited several successful compilations: *Harbinger: poetry and fiction by Los Angeles writers; Indivisible: short fiction by West Coast gay and lesbian writers; Blood Whispers: L.A. Writers on AIDS,* Volumes 1 and 2; the Lambda Literary Award-winning *His: brilliant new fiction by gay men* and *Hers: brilliant new fiction by lesbians,* volumes 1, 2, and 3 (with Robert Drake); the series *Circa 2000: Lesbian Fiction At the Millennium* and *Gay Fiction At the Millennium* (with Robert Drake); a poetry anthology, *Mischief, Caprice, and Other Poetic Strategies,* and the electronic book, *From Site to Vision: the Woman's Building in Contemporary Culture* (with Sondra Hale).

A performance artist in the 1970s and 80s, Wolverton has collaborated with choreographer Heidi Duckler and Collage Dance Theater on the site-specific performances *subVersions, Under Eden, After Eden,* and *Cover Story.* She is currently working with composer David Ornette Cherry on the adaptation of *Embers* as a jazz opera.

Terry has taught creative writing since 1977; in 1997, she founded Writers at Work, a center for creative writing in Los Angeles, where she offers several weekly workshops in fiction and poetry. She is also Associate Faculty Mentor in the MFA Writing Program of Antioch University Los Angeles.

She spent thirteen years at the Woman's Building, a public center for women's culture, eventually serving as its executive director. She is the recipient of numerous grants and awards for her artistic and community contributions, most recently, a California Arts Council Artist Fellowship for Poetry and a COLA Fellowship from the Los Angeles Department of Cultural Affairs.

She is also a certified instructor of Kundalini Yoga.

Find out more at www.terrywolverton.xbuild.com.

other books by terry wolverton

FICTION
Stealing Angel
The Labrys Reunion
Bailey's Beads

NONFICTION
Insurgent Muse: life and art at the Woman's Building

POETRY
Shadow and Praise
Embers, a novel in poems
Mystery Bruise
Black Slip

www.ingramcontent.com/pod-product-compliance
Lightning Source LLC
Chambersburg PA
CBHW070750120626
46557CB00002B/525